BACK IN THE SADDLE

BACHELOR AUCTION - BOOK 2

VANESSA VALE

GET A FREE VANESSA VALE BOOK!

Join Vanessa's mailing list to be the first to know of new releases, free books, special prices and other author giveaways.

http://freeromanceread.com

1

 ARAH

Friday night

One tug of his fingers on the tie at my waist, and the wrap dress came undone. His knuckles brushed my bare skin and I shivered. Not from cold but desire. The light material slid open and revealed my matching bra and panties.

"This is my new favorite kind of dress," Huck murmured, his head dipped, his gaze on my body. His sandy hair was thick and curly, and I wanted to reach out and run my fingers through it. Yet I held still. I tried to catch my breath because he'd barely touched me and I was hot for him. The way his pale eyes darkened, the way his jaw clenched... he wanted me. I also couldn't miss the thick prod of his dick against the front of his jeans. My pussy clenched, remembering how he'd felt inside me. We'd been in love, foolish, and—

"Baby girl, you're even more beautiful than I remember." His gaze flicked up. Met mine. Held. "And I remember often."

Baby girl.

I hadn't been called that in years, and only by Huck. Not since he broke up with me right before I left for college. I'd missed the endearment, along with him. The words reminded me it really was Huck Manning standing in front of me. Touching me. Hard for me.

Was I crazy doing this? The last time he'd had me —not only the last, but the first—I'd had my heart in on it. I'd loved him. Given him everything, including my virginity. I'd craved him and all he'd promised.

I wasn't nineteen any longer. Didn't have blinders on where he was concerned. I stood before him. Older. Wiser.

Still... this was Huck. I was in his bedroom, and I was close to naked. To hide my shaking hands, I raised them to his chest and gripped the cotton of his shirt. With a bold tug, the snaps gave way, revealing his broad torso.

He'd changed in six years. Filled out. Built muscle. His skin was tanned from the summer sun. His chest had a smattering of blond hair between dusky, flat nipples. When my fingertips brushed over his belly, his abs tightened.

"Fuck," he murmured, then took my wrist in a gentle hold.

I looked up, wondered why he stopped me.

The corner of his mouth curled. "Keep doing that and we'll be done too fast. I want this to last."

"Just touching you?" I whispered, awe in my voice. Not because he might have a quick trigger, but because I felt the power I had over him.

"Yeah, just the brush of your fingertips could finish me." His hand gently squeezed, and I looked up at him through my lashes. "We need to talk about this before we—"

I shook my head. The last thing I wanted to do was talk. I had a mission here. I had to stay focused on it. His touch... fuck, just his scent was making me lose my mind. He wasn't the only one who could come from just a a brush of his fingers. My clit ached and my pussy clenched with anticipation. My pussy wasn't in charge here though.

"No talking," I whispered.

He released his hold, his hands sliding up my arms to my shoulders, where he pushed my dress back. It slid silently to the floor so I was only in my underwear and cowgirl boots.

He took a step back, looked me over. I tried not to squirm, because it had been a really long time. I wasn't a teenager any longer. I'd filled out. He was too intense, his gaze heated. This was how he'd looked at me earlier across the crowded auditorium at the community center when I'd shouted out my bid at the bachelor auction.

It had only grown more intense once I'd won him and he'd hopped from the stage to join me in the crowd. To take my hand and lead me out of the building. To where we were now in his bedroom on the ranch with only a few articles of clothing between us.

It was as if he could stand it no longer and reached out, hooked a hand behind the back of my neck, and pulled me in. Kissed me.

Oh yes. This. I remembered his taste. The slightly rough feel of his hold. His barely leashed need. The gentle scrape of his stubble.

I pulled the tails of his shirt from his jeans as we kissed, my hands roaming now. His chest, his back, his butt over the denim.

He yanked me into him so I felt every hard inch. I was reminded of his size, a foot taller than my five-two. He could overpower me. Dominate me in ways that weren't kinky or fun.

But he wouldn't. The guy may have hurt my heart,

but I knew he'd never lay a hand on me in anger. In his arms was the one place where I'd felt truly safe.

Now I was back in them, and it was as if the six years slipped away.

With an arm banded around my back, he lifted me, carried me to the bed, and laid me down so my head rested on his pillow. With a hand pressed into the mattress by my shoulder, he loomed over me. With the glow of the bedside lamp, his face was cast in deep shadow. I saw the gleam of need. The happiness.

Lowering his head again, he kissed along my jaw, down my neck, and to the swell of my breast above the lacy edge of my bra.

A whimper slipped from my lips, and I tangled my fingers in his hair. Tugged on the silky strands. I remembered his scent, like coming home.

My eyes slipped closed at the delicious feel of him.

What was I doing? I couldn't lose myself in his touch!

I had a plan. A mission. But fuck, he felt so good. He remembered exactly what got me hot.

But he also knew exactly what had finished us.

I gripped the sides of his head and pulled him up. With a lift of my hips, I tried to flip us. He was too big to force, but he let me take the lead, rolling him onto his back as I straddled his waist.

His eyes flared with heat, and a slow smile spread across his face.

"Want to be in charge, baby girl?" he asked.

The fact that he asked proved that I really wasn't in charge at all. But I already was. He just didn't know it. I arched a brow and gave him a sly smile in return. "I did buy you at the auction."

His hands settled on my hips, the pads of his thumbs caressing my lower belly.

He was calm, relaxed. Content, even. He wanted me in his bed with him. Was pleased with it. With *me.*

I swallowed back all the feelings that knowledge brought about.

"Yeah, you did," he murmured. "You want a wild ride? I'll give you what you paid for."

I'd forgotten he was a dirty talker and seemed to only have gotten better at it. While we'd dated for a few months, we'd only been together, had sex, once. One night where he'd touched me in ways I'd never imagined. Never forgot.

But I'd been naive and unsure of what to do. He'd been gentle and careful. Obviously he liked this bolder version of me.

I shook my head—to tell him no and to clear the lust-filled haze—and looked to the chair in the corner of the room. Slung over the back of it was his utility belt. I climbed off him, went and grabbed the handcuffs. As police chief, he also had a service pistol, but it wasn't in the holster. Since he had a small child living in the house, I had no doubt it was stored in a gun safe along with any other weapons the Mannings had at the ranch.

I dangled the metal restraints from one finger as I stood before him.

"You want to be tied up, baby girl?" he asked, his eyes darkening at the idea.

I shook my head. "No. I want to do it to you."

His jaw clenched as he stared at me, looked me over as if memorizing me. "Fuck, you're beautiful."

He undid his jeans, pushed them and his boxers down over his hips so his dick sprang free. Only his shirt and pants were open; otherwise he still had his clothes on.

It was my turn to ogle him. I'd seen his dick before when we'd fooled around, touched it. Felt it deep inside me that one time. But I'd been young and a virgin then. I hadn't known how incredible Huck's dick actually was. Long, thick, and hard like it was, the crown flared wide. A little drop of pre-cum beaded at the tip. He gripped the base, gave it a rough stroke. Then he raised his hands over his head and gave me a wink.

"I'm all yours, baby girl."

I took a deep breath. I wanted to straddle him and sink deep onto him. Ride him like a cowgirl. But that wasn't the plan. This was Huck Manning. The guy who'd taken my virginity, told me he loved me, then dumped me. He'd taken my heart but left me with a part of him. That had died too, along with my hopes and dreams of being with him forever.

I'd follow through with my plan, and that meant going back to the bed and straddling him once again, panties staying on. Leaning forward, I grabbed one of his wrists and wrapped the cuff around, snapped it closed.

I gasped when Huck's mouth enclosed my nipple. The way I leaned over, I'd offered the lace-covered tip to him. I took a moment to enjoy the feel of the hot suck.

"Huck," I whispered, pleasure shooting from my nipple right to my clit.

He dropped his head back onto the pillow. Grinned.

I took another deep breath. My panties were drenched, and my clit pulsed with the need to come.

I quickly hooked the cuffs around a slat in his headboard, then affixed his other wrist. He gave a gentle tug to test them, and I smiled down at him.

Just how I wanted him.

"Before you take my dick for a ride, straddle my face. I want to eat that pussy before I take it hard."

Oh. My. God.

I stared at him. Those dark eyes were filled with lust, but honesty too. He wanted exactly what he'd said.

"I never got a taste before."

Because you dumped me.

It was time to leave him here, unsatisfied and unfucked, but Huck Manning was offering to go down on me. I'd been with two guys since Huck left me, but they hadn't been all that great. College boys who needed a road map and a compass to find my clit.

The guy beneath me was *all* man, and I had no doubt his confidence was earned.

He wanted to eat my pussy? Hell, I wasn't going to deny myself this opportunity for a man-induced orgasm, especially since he was restrained and couldn't do anything else.

Shifting, I stripped off my panties, then gripped the headboard to move over his face.

"Will you be able to breathe?" I asked, looking down at him. I wanted to punish him, not suffocate the guy.

Huck's gaze flicked from my pussy to my face. "Baby girl, it'll be the best way to go. Now lower down on my face."

He didn't say more because I shifted, and even without his hands, he went to town. Licking, flicking, sucking, kissing.

I rolled my hips, using the gorgeous Huck Manning to get off.

Oh. My. God. He was good. *This* was good. Too good.

It took about sixty seconds to gasp and cling to the

headboard as the best orgasm ever washed over me. I wasn't sure if it showed his skill as a lover or the fact that I'd been so desperate to come.

My nipples were pebbled, my skin slick with sweat. I shifted back, caught my breath as Huck licked his glistening lips.

"Not done," he said, his voice deep with arousal. "Grab a condom, climb on my dick, and let's have some fun."

I blinked. Looked down at Huck. I wanted to have sex with him. Desperately. It would be empty pleasure, though. He'd hurt me long ago. The wound had cut deep, and as I looked down at him, I knew it had never healed. I wasn't going to do that to myself again.

Revenge was sweet, especially when it came with an orgasm.

I climbed off him, grabbed my panties, and slipped them on. "No, thanks."

He didn't say anything, only frowned as he watched me pull my dress back on.

"Baby girl, what're you doing?"

"What I should have done all those years ago."

I picked up my purse from the floor, pulled out the piece of paper I'd found earlier, walked over, and slapped it onto his bare chest.

He looked down at it, then at me. "I kinda can't see what that is."

"It's a letter from a lawyer stating that Claire's not biologically yours," I explained.

His eyes flared at my words, and the cuffs clanged as he tugged against them. Yeah, he knew what I was talking about, but he hadn't expected it here and now. Just like that bit of news had been for me earlier when I'd pulled his lawyer's things from the totaled car.

"Sarah," he said, the first time he'd used my name tonight.

"You lied to me. For years." Anger laced my words. "You let me believe you had a baby with another woman."

"I can explain." The handcuffs rattled again as he tried to get himself free.

"No need," I said, holding up my hand. "Fuck you, Huckleberry Manning." I glanced at his still-hard dick. "Actually, I don't want to."

I turned on my heel and walked out of his room. Out of his life once again as I heard him shout my name. This time it was on my terms.

$\mathcal{H}$UCK

TWELVE HOURS earlier - Friday morning

"Is what Graham told me true, Lettuce?" I asked, sliding back the curtain around a gurney in the emergency room.

I set my hand on the butt of my gun at my hip as I looked Kale Bradford over. When I'd heard he'd been in an accident, I'd panicked but had been reassured his injuries were minor. So when I came to the ER to check on him, I fucked with him. As usual. I never let him live it down that he'd been named after a leafy green. We'd grown up together, surviving middle school growth spurts and high school fuckups without breaking a sweat. We'd been little assholes who'd grown into bigger assholes before we got our shit together in our early twenties. Kale had gone to law school, and I'd gone into the police academy. Now we enforced the law instead of trying to figure out ways to bend it.

A nurse passed, and I gave her a nod. I was here often enough for work to know most of the staff.

"Completely true. Can't make this shit up," he said, grinning as he tried to shift. He was propped up on a gurney in a hospital gown, an IV tube sticking out of his forearm and leading to a bag hung on a hook beside his head. His hairy lower legs and bare feet hung off the edge. His arm was in a sling, and there was a bandage on his forehead.

"A cow?" I asked, slowly shaking my head. "How is it possible you didn't avoid a cow in the middle of the road?"

He frowned, then winced again. "Fucker, . I avoided the fucking cow. That's why I'm here. He was in the middle of the curve on Old Thompkins Road. Since the curve was occupied, I went straight."

"Heard your truck's totaled."

He rolled his eyes. "Better the truck than me."

I'd had enough death in my life. I saw it often on the job, unfortunately. I didn't need my friend to bite it, especially because of a fucking cow. "Damn straight. Probably one of the Zinke's animals. The land to the north is all alfalfa."

I'd grown up here, knew what was going on in and around town.

"These drugs are good," he murmured, his eyes closing.

"They keeping you overnight?" He didn't look too banged up, but what did I know?

"A couple of hours. The hot nurse with the pink scrubs said they're not giving me any more of the pain meds through the IV." His eyes opened, and he tapped the tube that led to the bag. "I fucking have to piss."

I went over, took his arm, and helped him stand. He gripped the IV pole, and we walked to the bathroom, his ass hanging out. "Please tell me you can take a leak on your own."

He looked to me, his dark eyes, blurry from the pain meds, narrowed. "If I want someone to hold my dick for me, it'll be the nurse in pink."

I held up my hands to tell him I was backing off, then leaned against the wall outside the bathroom to wait.

He came out a minute later. "As your lawyer, I'm telling you you've got a problem with Mandy. She's not going away, and based on the phone call from *her* lawyer that accompanied the letter in my briefcase, she's batshit crazy. I guess he's been paid so far in cash but is doing this for the big payout when she wins."

I had no idea what he'd done in the crapper, but he came out all business, even if he walked back to the gurney at the pace of an eighty-year-old. I didn't like anything he said. Mandy had been crazy enough to lie to me because she wanted my cash and was now back. That meant she was probably crazier than ever.

"I'll do whatever it takes to protect Claire."

"Mandy's her mom, and she's threatening to exercise that right. She wants custody."

Like that was ever going to fucking happen.

I'd met Mandy when I was in Helena at the police academy. I'd been twenty-four, and she'd lived in the same crappy apartment building. She'd been a hot fucking mess, to put it nicely. Drugs. Random men. Shouting matches with them at all hours of the day and night. It had been annoying, but I'd been angry and dealing with having to walk away from Sarah. If I wasn't at the academy, I drank. Often I'd pass out. Black out even.

One morning she'd been in my kitchen making me eggs. Said we'd fucked. I hadn't remembered a thing, but with how out of control I'd been, it hadn't been all that surprising. Horrible and a stupid fucking mistake since Sarah had been the only one I'd wanted. The fact that I'd been one of Mandy's random hookups had been the wake-up call I'd needed for the way I'd dealt with a broken heart. I'd dumped all the whiskey down the drain, carted the empties to the recycling, and gotten tested for any and all STDs. I'd been clean, but three weeks later Mandy had knocked on my door and told me she was pregnant. With my kid.

It had taken a while—a fucking understatement— to come to terms with the fact that I was going to have a baby, and not with Sarah as I'd always imagined. I'd broken up with Sarah because I'd had to, but it hadn't gone down easy. And then I'd fucked it up even more.

Mandy hadn't been the model pregnant woman. She hadn't changed her ways at all. Partying. Men. When her actions had endangered my unborn kid, I'd stepped in. She'd lost her shit, and I knew if I was going to get her out of the picture, I needed to use every bit of what I'd learned at the academy to my advantage. I took pictures. Video of her less-than-motherly behavior.

She'd had the baby without ever having called me. I'd shown up at the hospital and overheard her tell a friend I wasn't the father and she'd been playing me all along. We hadn't even fucked like she'd said. It was then I pulled out my evidence, called Kale, and forced her to terminate her rights and give me full custody. Fifty thousand also sweetened the pot. She'd walked out of that hospital less than twenty-four hours after having Claire, paperwork signed, and never looked back.

I became a daddy to a baby that wasn't mine, officially confirmed later by a paternity test. But one look at newborn Claire and there had been no going back. I hadn't cared whose DNA she carried. I'd thought she was mine for months, and I was keeping her.

I'd finished the academy and returned to The Bend with a newborn. My child.

Five years later Claire thrived on the ranch. I might not have been the sperm donor, but I was her father. Only Kale, my brothers Sawyer and Thatcher, and Alice, our housekeeper, knew the truth.

I hadn't heard from Mandy in all this time. "She's not here for custody. She never wanted Claire. Hasn't been involved in her life one fucking bit. Why now?"

He looked to me, shifted, and winced. "Cash, probably."

I sighed, ran a hand over the back of my neck. It was the Manning money she was after. The family ranch was huge. Me and my brothers were set for life between the land and the inheritance from our parents. But we worked for a living. Mannings were never idle.

"If she knows where to find me, even through you, she knows I'm chief of police. Not the best person to extort."

He dropped his head back on the stiff pillow. "I didn't say she was smart, but she does have Claire's DNA."

"I'll pay her if it keeps Claire safe and happy."

Kale shifted. "Yeah, well. You did that once and she's back. Her lawyer sent papers that outlined that you're not Claire's biological father and she'll fight for custody."

"Unless..."

"Unless you pay her more. Child support."

"How does she have money for a lawyer?" I wondered.

His head rocked back and forth in a pseudo-head-shake. That made him close his eyes for a second. "She doesn't. Like I said, he wrote a letter, nothing more. Maybe a hundred bucks. The real payout's from you."

I laughed and ripped the curtain back a little more. "I'm the one supporting the child. Jesus," I muttered. Claire was mine. She deserved a life without Mandy in it. She'd only ruin her. I couldn't even imagine my sweet blonde-haired child with that crazy bitch. I thanked God often I'd gotten her away from that woman. Claire was off to kindergarten in the fall. Smart as a whip. My little cowgirl. The only thing she might be missing in her life was a front tooth and a mama.

I ran a hand over my face. Sighed. "I'll call Mandy. Go see her tonight and make it clear she has no case."

"The bachelor auction's tonight," he reminded me. "Not sure whose wrath is worse, Mandy or Alice."

It was my turn to grimace at how my housekeeper would respond if I didn't show. Kale had practically grown up on the ranch with me and my brothers and knew Alice well. "Fine. I'll call her instead. Make a visit some other time."

I'd been informed the on Wednesday I was to be in the fundraiser that was at the community center tonight. Alice had volunteered me along with Sawyer and Thatcher for the event. Kale was one of the bachelors as well, but he obviously was out now. The event and cause were a good one, but I wasn't interested in dating. I had a kid, and I wasn't bringing just any woman around Claire.

I thought of Sarah O'Banyon. Long blonde hair that I used to capture with my fingers. Full lips that turned pink and swollen from my kisses. Small breasts that fit my palms perfectly. A pussy that I'd sunk into and found heaven on earth.

I'd thought she would be mine, every inch of her... until her dad threatened me. Told me I was a punk, partying and drinking, not giving much of a shit about anything since my parents had died. All of that had been true. Sarah had deserved more, he said. Her older sister, Lynn, had been dating Bunky at the time, and her dad had used her as a comparison. They were married now, and if what the rumor mill said was true, it was far from a happy marriage.

Bill O'Banyon had wanted Sarah to go to college and make something of herself. Something better than to be with a little shit like me. His words had hit their mark because he'd been right. I had been a little shit. But not to Sarah. She'd been the only person to see past my wild ways to my hurt. To my grieving.

I'd been man enough to stand up to him all those years ago, defending what Sarah and I had, until he said he'd cut her off and not pay for her college.

I'd laughed because with the Manning money, I could give Sarah anything she ever wanted.

Except her father himself.

And that was where I'd stopped the fight. I'd had to walk away. It had been a fucking nightmare, lying through my teeth to her, breaking both our hearts because her dad was a dick. Because he'd tossed out the one ultimatum I couldn't fight.

I'd lost my parents in a plane crash when I was fourteen. I knew what it was like without a father. I wanted to be Sarah's family, but she needed more than me.

So I'd walked. Let her go to college. I'd gone to the academy with the hopes of being worthy of her love.

Until Mandy and then Claire.

When Sarah had returned from her first year at college, I'd had a newborn. To Sarah and the entire town, I'd moved on. No one wanted the truth. They'd assumed. I'd hoped, perhaps stupidly, that Sarah would come to me after she saw I'd pulled my shit together. But she hadn't.

I'd wanted Sarah, but Claire was my *child*.

After all this time, Sarah was the one I wanted... and I wasn't sure if that said how sad of a fucker I was or if what I'd felt for her was the only real love I was ever going to know.

"The only way to get out of the auction is to be like me." Kale lifted his non-IV'd arm to point at his head. "Avoid a cow."

"I'll deal with Mandy," I said on a sigh. "And show up for the auction. I have to go track down a loose cow before anyone else gets hurt. Then I've got to pick up Claire from her school's summer camp."

"Tell her Uncle Kale will take her to the library next week."

I huffed out a laugh at their usual date activity. "Maple had puppies. I think you're low on her list right now."

He gave a look of mock horror. "My favorite girl blinded by puppies? I'll stop by then. She can show them off. Might even pick one for myself. My papers and other things are still in my truck. Graham said he'd get it towed and have my briefcase at the station for me. Can you check on that? Because I don't want it going to the junkyard before it's cleaned out."

"Anything else? For a guy laid up because of a cow, you're pretty needy."

He gave me the middle finger. Yeah, he was going to be fine. I gave him the bird right back and left the ER. I had shit to do, including tracking down a damned cow.

3

 ARAH

FRIDAY AFTERNOON

I PULLED the flatbed tow truck over to the side of the road just past where the older pickup had stopped in the field. It was clear it had missed the turn and gone straight into the alfalfa, taking the wire fencing and a post with it. Even from where I sat, I could see the front axle was bent so bad one of the tires was facing sideways. The front bumper was at the base of the ditch, ripped off when the truck had hit nose-first.

Before I turned off the engine, I noticed on the

dash that the tow truck's temperature gauge was a little high. Closing my eyes for a second, I mentally swore at Roy and my dad for ignoring the coolant. I pushed open the door and jumped down from the seat, grabbing my work gloves.

Graham Armstrong was the deputy on scene. The only one, in fact, who remained to wait for me. He approached, offering an easy smile. I'd gone to school with his younger sister, who had the same red hair. "Surprised to see you here," he said. "You don't usually go out on calls."

I frowned because while he was making only small talk, he'd struck a nerve. It was true. While my father called O'Banyon Auto Shop a family business, all I usually touched were the books. My father wouldn't let me touch the cars, whether on an accident like this or in one of the three repair bays in the shop. At least, not if he was around. I did, on occasion, without him knowing, when one of the guys who worked for him wasn't available. These days it was only Dad and Roy, the other mechanic.

I'd graduated with my business degree but had stayed in Bozeman for my accountant certification, finally returning to The Bend at twenty-three. Now I ran my own bookkeeping business, handling the paperwork for a number of companies in town. This included tackling the billing, accounts, and all things behind-the-scenes for my father. I used modern software and a computer, although Dad gave me his paperwork usually in a shoebox or a stack of bills and invoices on his desk. He didn't care about the business aspect and it showed. He relied on me for it. Always had since I was in middle school.

Even though I was a number cruncher, I knew my way around an engine. And a tow truck. I'd been able to fix a carburetor when I was eleven. My friends had compared me to Mona Lisa Vito, the wife from the film *My Cousin Vinny,* who knew everything about cars. I'd always wanted to be like my dad and be a mechanic and run a shop. Since winters were long in Montana, I'd spent a lot of free time reading, learning, and puttering. Even now I had my own tools in the one-car garage connected to my house to work on things, like my vintage Jeep and my neighbor's lawn mower.

I wanted to run the shop *with* my dad. Take it over when he retired. He'd always been resistant to the idea, which annoyed me. He'd been pushing me off, again and again. Fortunately my accounting business was busy and my bank account filled, which kept me from grumbling too much. He was stringing me along, and up until now I'd been okay with it. Lately I'd been unsettled, ready to hash it out one way or the other. Especially since Roy was a no-show. Again.

But even if I wanted to strike out on my own, I couldn't open a repair shop in such a small town, especially if my father was the competition. He needed me.

He just didn't want to admit it. Doing so would mean I'd been right... that while I'd always wanted to go to college, I also wanted to fix cars.

I tipped my sunglasses up onto the top of my head. "My dad's at Sturgis. Gets back later today or tomorrow, I think."

Graham nodded in understanding. The huge motorcycle rally in South Dakota was a motorcyclist's annual mecca and one my dad never missed. He'd been gone all week. "Where's Roy?"

I tried not to frown. "No idea. I'm guessing still in bed."

I filled in for him often enough. Knew he was a hard partier and a hard drinker. I'd have fired him a while ago, but my father didn't see an issue. Except he didn't know I covered. It was the only way to get my hands beneath a hood at the shop and the only way the place was going to stay in business.

"You told your pop that?" The question indicated that Graham knew my dad and his personality. Gruff and old-fashioned. Stuck in his ways. Stuck in his ways about *me*.

I laughed, tugged my second glove on. "Hell, no."

When I argued that was what I wanted to do with my life, he'd tossed up his hands and pointed out that my sister, Lynn, had listened to him. Found a better life than a blue-collar mechanic's daughter.

Lynn was married to Tom Bunker, known around

town as Bunky, and had two kids. She was miserably unhappy, but she was also shallow. She stuck it out because her husband was rich and she liked expensive things more than a loving spouse.

Turning, I set my hands on my hips and checked out the wreck. I was done talking about my screwed-up family dynamics. "What happened here?" I asked, although it was pretty obvious.

Graham pointed and I turned to look in that direction.

"The cow?" One dark cow stood eating grass on the side of the road. Only prairie and big sky was behind her.

"It was Kale Bradford versus the Hereford."

I glanced back at the truck. "Looks like the Hereford won. Is Kale okay?" I hadn't seen the guy in a long time. Not since Huck and I had dated, as they were best friends.

"He's fine. A little beat-up."

"The truck's not," I said. "That axle damage is enough for any insurance company to total it."

Graham scratched the back of his neck. The sun was warm, and it felt good to be away from my desk and balancing a spreadsheet. "That's my thinking."

"I'm on it. I'll get it loaded up so you can do something besides stand on the side of the road."

He gave a shrug, then checked his watch. "The bachelor auction's tonight. Gotta go spiff up."

I spun on my booted heel and eyed the guy up and down. "Some woman's going to empty her bank account for you."

He blushed as red as his hair, then swiped his fingernails over his uniform shirt as if buffing them. Graham was a nice guy. Sweet. Caring. He'd make a fine husband, but not mine. I'd been off men for a long time. Too long. My friends said I had cobwebs on my vagina. Sadly it had been a while.

"Maybe I should buy myself a guy," I said to him, joking. Although if I was going to get back in the dating game, this was one way to do it.

"The Mannings are up for sale." His chin was tipped down, and he gave me a cautious look. Butterflies danced around in my stomach at the mention of the Manning boys. My mind went to one in particular.

Tall, blond, gorgeous. He had a quick smile that could make any woman hand him her panties. I knew that for a fact.

"Huck Manning had his chance and walked away," I said, frowning. Graham knew exactly what I was talking about. So did everyone in town, even though it was old news. "I think Claire Manning's proof of that." I shrugged and tried to play it off. "Thatcher and Sawyer aren't hard on the eyes though."

"If that's all you're looking for, check out this face right here." He pointed at himself.

I burst out laughing, and so did he.

Carefully I worked my way down the embankment to Kale's truck. While the driver's door had a dent, it opened easily. Papers were strewn across the bench seat, and I pushed them away to climb behind the wheel. I needed to get in to put the vehicle in neutral so it would roll when the winch pulled it onto the flatbed. I grabbed the gearshift and got it into the right gear, but the papers caught my eye. I collected them all into a pile to stick back into the briefcase that had obviously opened in the crash. The top paper looked like a legal document—Kale Bradford *was* a lawyer— but it was Huck Manning's name that caught my attention.

I had to take a guess, since they were best friends, that Kale was Huck's legal counsel. I shouldn't have snooped at something that was probably confidential, but when it had Huck's name on it, I didn't give a shit.

I skimmed it quickly, then started over, this time reading it slower. It was a letter from some lawyer in Helena for his client, an Amanda Oglethorpe of Helena. He stated that while Huck wasn't Claire Manning's biological father, he was currently the legal guardian of her. Amanda Oglethorpe was intending to take Huck to court for her maternal rights to be reinstated.

My heart skipped a beat, then another. My palms began to sweat. I glanced out the cracked windshield and didn't see the acres of growing alfalfa or the mountains in the distance. All I saw was Huck Manning, five years ago, coming back to The Bend with a baby. *His* baby.

The baby that proved he'd moved on and hadn't wanted me.

Huck Manning wasn't Claire's father. He hadn't dumped me and gone on to make a baby with a woman faster than someone changed their underwear.

He'd made one with me, but—

"Everything okay?" Graham asked, making me jump. I set the paper beside me.

I'd been so lost in my thoughts I hadn't heard him approach.

Hastily I picked up the small pile and grabbed the open briefcase off the floor of the passenger side. "Yeah, these were all over and in my way." I shoved them in, except for the one letter about Huck, and snapped the lid down. Reaching across the steering wheel, I handed the briefcase to Graham through the open door. "Here. I'm sure Kale's going to want this."

He took it from me. "I'll see that he gets it. Thanks."

With the truck ready to be loaded, I hopped out and folded the letter, shoving it into the back pocket of my jeans. We walked to the tow truck together. As I readied the winch cable, all I could think about was what I'd just learned.

Huck and I had dated after graduation and spent the summer together, practically inseparable. God, it had been intense, and I'd fallen in love with him in a matter of days. Maybe on our first date. I'd given him my virginity the week before I was to leave for college.

The next day he'd come to the house and told me it was over. I'd sat there as he'd told me it wasn't going to work. My dad had stood in the doorway and watched. His face had been grim as usual. He'd never been shy in how he felt about Huck Manning. While I'd been heartbroken, my dad had consoled me by telling me I was better than a loser like Huck, that he'd never amount to anything, that he'd drag me down.

I hadn't believed any of it, but Huck hadn't changed his mind. I'd gone off to college and tried to heal my broken heart. Until I found out I was pregnant. Until a short while later I'd miscarried.

I'd heard Huck had moved to Helena to go to the police academy, but he'd never contacted me, so I never told him about the baby we'd made. The loss of him and the miscarriage had made that first year horrible. But I'd persevered. College was what I'd wanted. What my father had always planned for me. To amount to more, although by then all I'd wanted was the life Huck and I had begun to plan. That was never going to be.

When school ended for the year, I'd returned to The Bend for the summer. Huck had too. With a baby. With little Claire.

Since I was good with numbers, I'd done the math,

figured he'd gone from taking my virginity in the back of his truck to another woman's bed within a month. Proven we were truly finished.

It had taken years to get over him. The way I was reacting to this news, I wasn't past him at all.

He'd returned to The Bend and worked as a deputy, raising Claire on his own. He had Alice, the awesome Manning housekeeper, and two brothers to help, but never once reached out to me. I'd had to hear all the gossip about it, the mystery of who the mother was. I'd had to listen to all the times my dad told me how much better off I was without him. How Claire had proved Huck Manning was a deadbeat, that he'd have ruined my life.

But now? Kale's papers? Claire wasn't Huck's baby. Why had he lied? Why had he let me believe she was his, that he'd slept with another woman so soon after me? That I'd meant so little to him that he'd found another. That he'd gotten her pregnant.

I was so angry as I let out the cable on the winch. Graham grabbed the end and went to hook it beneath the front of Kale's pickup.

I willed the tears away. I'd grieved not only the end of our relationship but the baby I'd thought we'd made in love. Had to see Claire Manning and know the child we'd created would have been exactly her age. That she could have been ours. Together.

I had to confront Huck. I had to know the truth.

But first I was going to get even. How dare he lie to me about something like that! How dare he think so little of me. He'd turned his life around, proving to the entire town he was a stand-up guy. A leader in the community who gave back.

It had been six years. I'd thought I was done with him. If I was, I wouldn't be losing my shit over the paperwork. But no. It cut deep. So deep.

I flipped the lever to tilt the truck bed.

"Think I should wear a blue shirt or a green one tonight?" Graham asked, stirring me from my thoughts once again.

"Green," I told him, pushing the button for the winch and watching as the cable went taut and slowly began to pull the truck across the field. I took a deep breath, let it out. Tried to calm down, but my heart was practically beating out of my chest. "With that hair, the women are going to go wild."

He took off his hat and watched as Kale's truck slid into position on the flatbed. I stopped the winch, then lowered the bed back down so it was flat.

I needed to talk to Huck. Now. I stilled, then smiled. I knew a way to do just that. I'd get the answers I wanted. And then some.

$\mathcal{H}$UCK

THATCHER and I were the only two bachelors left to be auctioned off. Sawyer had just gone. I leaned against the wall backstage as he was bid on, not wanting to know how he fared. It was like waiting for our turn for the guillotine.

Alice had volunteered us, so it wasn't like we could duck out from the event now by taking the nearest emergency exit. She'd kill us and with a dull knife. In our sleep. The last person I wanted mad at me was

Alice. She'd been the Manning Ranch housekeeper longer than I'd been alive and mother hen for me and my brothers since my parents had died.

I was first to admit that had been a hellish job. I'd been a punk when I was a kid, but after my parents' plane had crashed, I'd turned into a full-fledged asshole. For years.

I sighed, because I knew the moment I'd turned my shit around. When Sarah O'Banyon's dad had forced me to walk away. When he'd said I wasn't good enough for his daughter. Never had been, never would be.

It seemed I wasn't good enough for not just Sarah, but for any woman. I hadn't found one who'd stuck. Hell, who I'd wanted to stick. I hadn't taken one to the ranch or to meet Claire. Sure, I'd been able to separate a woman from her panties on occasion. That wasn't an issue, and definitely not one I shared with Alice. The family housekeeper wanted the three of us to settle down, to marry, not continue with random one-night stands.

Casual sex was one thing, but marriage? That was something else entirely. Something I'd wanted once. With Sarah. And since that was a dead fucking end, it was why I was here now. Waiting to be auctioned off to the highest bidding woman since I couldn't get one on my own. I'd probably make five dollars for the charity tonight.

I wanted forever, but no doubt get a coffee date at

the new place on Main with Miss Turnbuckle, the town's librarian. The one who'd looked eighty when I was a kid.

"Fuck," I grumbled to myself. I remembered how I'd felt for Sarah, the way she'd looked at me when I took her for the first time in the back of my pickup. How I'd loved her, wanted to worship every inch of her. Back then I'd gone from thinking only of myself to my sole goal in life being to make her happy.

The crowd of women in the audience screamed and clapped louder than ever. Something was happening, but it didn't sound like anyone needed law enforcement's intervention. Thatcher went over to the curtain that kept the backstage area from view and peeked out. I moved to stand beside him to see what the fuck was going on.

I caught a glimpse of Sawyer striding out of the auditorium, a woman tossed over his shoulder. I couldn't see who it was, but she had red hair. Lots of it.

Thatcher stepped back, grinned. "I didn't think Sawyer had it in him."

I took off my Stetson, ran a hand over my hair. Unbelievable. Sawyer wanted a woman enough to carry her from the auction. "Me either."

Sawyer was the serious one of the three of us. It was definitely because he was the oldest. He'd felt he had to take care of us since our parents died. Hell, he took care of everyone. That was why he was fire chief.

I took the other chief role in town. My reasons hadn't been so altruistic. My goal hadn't been to help other people when I'd come back from the academy and taken a deputy position. It had been to help *me*. To get Sarah to see me as worthy.

Five years in and even taking up the chief role, that hadn't happened.

Reverend Abernathy popped his head around the curtain. He was smiling and seemed quite pleased with himself. "Your brother had the highest bid of the night. Five hundred dollars!"

"Holy sh—" Thatcher said, then cut himself off and offered a shameful smile. "Sorry, Reverend."

The man held up his hand. "I am surprised as well. The money is for a good cause; therefore I think God would have to agree with you. This time, especially since you did make the shit holy." He gave Thatcher a pointed look, then grinned again. "Who's next?"

I looked to my brother. Even though he was an inch taller, he was still my little brother. Since he was the sole carrottop in the family for generations, I'd always teased him that he'd been adopted. The childhood teasing should have kept him up at night with doubt of his DNA, but everything rolled right off him. Even now he was the easygoing one.

"I'll go," I offered. No way in fuck was I going to stand back here all by myself. I'd feel like the last picked in middle school gym. If I was going to get back in the saddle, now was the fucking time.

The reverend nodded, then disappeared.

"Hope Miss Turnbuckle wins you," he said.

I tilted my chin and narrowed my eyes. "Why's that?"

"Then she won't bid on me."

I frowned, spun on my booted heel, and went out onstage when the minister introduced me. If anyone thought it strange a man of God was selling men to a crowd full of women, no one said. Especially not the crowd of over a hundred women.

I heard a few catcalls, some whistling.

"Ladies, it's time to bid on the date with the chief of police!"

Clapping ensued and someone shouted, "Will he bring the handcuffs?"

I pasted a smile on my face and rolled my eyes. I hadn't heard that one before... this week.

I was all for a little play in bed, but I was the aggressor. I was the one who put the cuffs on. Took charge and made a woman beg for release. And I didn't mean from the cuffs.

"Shall we start at fifty dollars?"

I scanned the crowd, the exit points, my usual survey of the room since it was my job to ensure everyone was safe.

"Five hundred dollars!"

I didn't even process what had been shouted until gasps and whispers spread across the room.

Reverend Abernathy chuckled. "I think I heard a lady say five hundred dollars?"

In the center of the room, a woman rose from one of the many round tables. "Five hundred dollars," she called again. This time I didn't take notice of anything but her.

Sarah O'Banyon. Petite, blonde. A hundred pounds soaking wet. Her blue eyes held mine. Her chin was raised in defiance.

I remembered every inch of this woman. The way her mouth turned up, the little dimple by her elbow, the small mole on the inside of her right thigh. The pale hair that framed her pink pussy.

I'd rarely seen her around town. Once in the grocery store, once on a call when her father had been down with the flu and needed someone to tow a car that had slid off the road. She was older now, not nineteen any longer. She'd filled out some, her breasts a little fuller, her hips a little wider.

Yet in the six years since I'd been with her last, in the back of my pickup under a starry sky, she'd never once looked me in the eye.

Until now.

Now she wouldn't look away.

She'd bid a shit ton of money. Hadn't even waited for the numbers to rise.

She knew what she wanted.

Me.

Yet I had no idea why. Why now?

Everyone else in the room knew it too. Anyone over the age of twenty most likely knew our history, and they had front-row seats for the latest bit of town gossip.

"Sold!" the reverend called, then laughed. When the clapping quieted down, he continued. "I don't think, ladies, that I should keep a woman from what she wants."

For once I was in complete agreement with the man of God. If Sarah O'Banyon wanted me, I was all fucking hers.

I didn't even nod at the reverend. Alice could scold me for it later. I didn't look away from Sarah, maybe afraid she'd disappear if I did, and hopped from the stage. Skirting around the tables, I made my way to stand in front of her. I took off my hat, dipped my chin so I could keep looking into those eyes as pale as mine.

"Is Reverend Abernathy right, baby girl? You want me?"

Her cheeks flushed, and she swallowed hard. "Yes."

That one word. Fuck, that one word was a gateway to everything.

Yes, I want you to finally make me yours.

Yes, I want to be with you always.

Yes, I love you, Huckleberry Manning.

I'd heard all those yeses from her. Remembered every single one. That one word was the key to my heart. I had no idea why Sarah had bid on me now, why she was looking at me like she had all those years ago, but this time, if I let her in, all she'd find was that my heart was broken.

And yet I was eager for her. For this and whatever was going to happen next. As I took her hand and led her out of the auditorium, I knew I wasn't going to be the same again. I wasn't sure if that was going to save me or destroy me.

Either way, she was mine. This time I wasn't fucking letting her go.

$\mathcal{H}$UCK

AN HOUR later

WHAT THE FUCK? I stared at my closed bedroom door. Sarah had just gotten dressed, covered up that gorgeous womanly body, and left me. After she'd dropped a fucking bombshell. I glanced down at the paper on my chest, but I couldn't read it. The handcuffs rattled as I yanked on them, but there was no give.

"Sarah!" I called, then snapped my mouth shut, grinding my molars together.

I still had her taste on my tongue, her sticky essence on my chin. I was aching to sink into her, my dick hard and throbbing against my lower belly. I'd almost busted a nut when her dress had slipped to the floor. Fuck, the sight of her in that pretty lingerie and soft, silky skin was something I'd always remember. The fact that she'd *let* me get beneath her dress meant she'd wanted me. I'd never touch her otherwise. That was why I'd stayed away all this time. She hadn't wanted me. If she had, she'd have come to me.

She had, but after six years.

Sarah O'Banyon was my every fantasy come to life. Had been since she turned eighteen. I'd wanted her all those years ago, and I still wanted her now. I hadn't been celibate since, but sex had been a release. To blow off some steam. Nothing more. Sarah'd had my heart once, and it had been destroyed.

I battled often with how I'd handled her dad. I should've told him to fuck off, then carry Sarah away on the back of my horse like some kind of sappy western. But he'd threatened to not only take away her college fund but disown her. He was an asshole, but I wouldn't risk Sarah's happiness for anything. So I'd stayed away.

I listened. The house was completely quiet. The crickets chirping through the open window were all I could hear.

She wasn't coming back. The breeze did nothing to

cool me down. My jeans were open, and my dick was out, hard and dripping pre-cum. I was handcuffed to the fucking headboard. The only person in the house was Alice—Claire was spending the night with one of her friends so all of us could attend the auction—and she was the dead-last person I wanted to come to my rescue.

It was one thing for everyone to learn about how Delilah had snuck through Sawyer's bedroom window all those years ago, but this? Now? I was thirty-two years old. No one needed to know I gotten hard being restrained.

Hell, I hadn't known I liked it until Sarah, in little scraps of lace and silk, dangled my cuffs from her finger.

"Fuck!" I growled, this time a hell of a lot softer.

She'd planned this. The seduction? Fake.

No. It hadn't been fake. She'd been dripping wet. Eager. She'd rolled her hips over my face as I ate her out. She'd come, and hard.

No fucking way she'd faked that.

She'd taken what she wanted, then left behind what she'd intended.

A hard dick and the paper on my chest.

Claire's not biologically yours.

She wasn't. I remembered the looks around town when I'd brought her home. The whispers. *Of course Huck Manning had knocked someone up. He was* never going to amount to anything, especially when he had a child out of wedlock and who knew what had happened with the mother. They wouldn't have believed the truth. They believed their *own* truth.

They hadn't deserved to know what really happened. How I'd saved Claire from being raised by a horrible mother.

Outside of my family, the only person I'd wanted to tell never once looked me up. I'd stupidly hoped she might. It hadn't mattered that I'd turned my life around, raised a girl I was fucking proud of. I was just the fuckup everyone said.

Years went by. The last person I'd thought to bid on me at the auction was Sarah O'Banyon. When she'd stood up in the crowd, I'd been stunned. Immediately I'd wondered… *why?* We hadn't said much after I tugged her out of the packed auditorium and to my truck. All she'd said was, *"Take me home."*

And I had.

Only three words and my dick had gone instantly hard. There had been a moment when I'd had clarity, when I'd stopped and told her we had to talk. We had too much unsaid between us, but she'd shut that down. She'd even said, *"No talking."*

Yeah, my dick had liked that. And taken over.

Fuck! I should've at least *tried* to think about the why of it all. But no. Sarah had always led me around by my dick, and she'd done it again. I wanted her. Still.

She still wanted me, too. But she wanted something else from me as well.

The truth.

The paper on my chest told it all.

I realized where she must have gotten it. Kale's accident. Her dad's shop was the only tow in town and the one we used for police matters. She worked for him, ran the business side of it. She must've collected Kale's things out of the truck, found the letter. Learned the truth. Wasn't happy about it.

Obviously, based on the fact that my balls were aching, she'd had a plan to get back at me.

Hell hath no fury like a woman scorned.

Sarah was scorned as shit.

Technically I'd broken up with her. But not by choice. I'd done it for *her.* I sighed, tipped my chin back, grabbed the wooden slat that held me prisoner, and tugged at it, but it didn't give. "Fucking quality construction," I grumbled to myself.

I wasn't sure how I was going to get out of this mess with my dignity intact. But that wasn't all that important now.

Sarah was what was important. I'd hurt her. Enough to buy me at an auction so she could get me like this, to punish me. Payback for what she thought I'd done to her. I tugged on the slat some more. Gritted my teeth and yanked.

She still had feelings for me, although not the right

ones. I had to make this right. She was out there mad at me. I couldn't have that. The thought that I'd hurt her again, that she'd been hurting all this time was like acid in my stomach.

There was hope though. I tasted it on my tongue.

She might hate my guts, but she wanted me. If I had to get her in my cuffs and pleasure her until she talked, I'd do it. It was time to get shit straightened out. To make her mine once and for all.

As soon as I got out of these fucking cuffs.

6

ARAH

"YOU *BOUGHT* HUCK MANNING?"

I stalled at my dad's question just outside the doorway to the service bay. Blinked.

Of course he would have heard about what I'd done at the auction. The Bend was small enough that word traveled fast. I hadn't been subtle about my interest in winning Huck Manning. I'd given the first and only bid and was going to be taking a chunk out of my checking account to pay for it.

No woman could blame me. He was over six feet of male perfection. Solid. Strong. Chiseled. Tousled fair hair I remembered running my fingers through. A square jaw I'd... sat on. His mouth. God, so skilled. He might be the chief of police, but he was dangerous to me.

I cut over to the shop's small kitchenette, pulled a mug from the cabinet, and peeked inside it to make sure it was actually clean, then filled it from the coffee pot, which was always fresh and full. Only after I doctored it with some sugar did I respond.

Dad flared quick to anger, faster than a brushfire across a dry prairie. Always had. At least ever since Mom left, which was when I'd been seven. I didn't remember much of her or my father before that other than her smile, her hugs. Her perfume.

I was used to his rough grumble and could handle him, but not before some caffeine.

I hadn't slept well, tossing and turning and thinking of Huck. Of how he'd gotten me off with just his mouth.

I'd never done that before, and I didn't mean seduce a guy into handcuffs. *That* I hadn't done either. I'd never had a guy go down on me, and I'd never imagined it happening by sitting on his face.

It had been hot. Too hot. I'd come so fast I was sure Huck was smug about the accomplishment. I tried not to think about how much I'd needed an orgasm, or that I'd wanted one still from Huck. My nipples were hard beneath my bra, and my pussy ached for that big cock I'd left thick, long and ready for me.

My plan had been to seduce him into being cuffed to his bed. I'd imagined leaving my clothes on. Maybe kiss him. When he'd undone my dress, I'd liked it. When he'd kissed me, I'd really liked it. Then I'd gotten him locked to the bed as I'd wanted, and I *still* hadn't walked away. Not after he'd offered to get me off.

I'd figured I owed it to women everywhere to follow through with that.

And boy, had I.

Sex hadn't been part of my revenge plan. I didn't do vengeful sex, and having it with him—or any guy— was just... wrong.

But riding Huckleberry Manning's face to have the best orgasm of my life? Hell, yeah.

Propping a hip against the chipped counter, I blew on the black coffee, then took a careful sip.

"Well?" Dad stood just inside the bay, wiping his hands on an old rag as his rough growl echoed. The garage doors were open to the warm weather, and he was silhouetted by the bright sunshine. He was in his old coveralls. They used to be navy but had faded with all the washing and had indeterminate stains down the front. His hair was long and pulled back into a thin ponytail. The dark color had streaks of gray cutting through and the hairline was receding at a swift pace.

"You heard it from someone, so why do you need to ask me?" I wasn't sure why I was giving him sass. All it did was rile him up. But I wasn't fifteen. I was a grown woman and didn't need him meddling.

He narrowed his eyes. "Because I want to hear it from you."

"I bought Huck Manning," I replied.

"You're not a kid any longer." Yet he was still sticking his nose in. "I thought you'd grown out of being stupid where that punk is concerned."

His words were jam-packed with so much insult. I didn't miss any of it, felt it deep down, but I didn't let it show. *That* was worse than riling him.

"He's the chief of police," I countered. "I'd say he's not much of a punk any longer." It wasn't that I was defending Huck as much as defending my ability to make my own decisions.

He frowned. "Trust me. I know guys like him."

"Okay," I replied, turning to head to the small office in the back.

I heard his deep sigh. "Pumpkin."

His usual endearment had me pausing. He hadn't pulled that one out in a while because... yeah, I was twenty-six.

"Why did you do it? After what he did?"

What he did was take my virginity and then came by and told me it wasn't going to work, that I was headed to college in Bozeman and he shouldn't hold me back. Nothing I'd said in return had swayed him. We were over, and that was it.

I shrugged, took a sip of the coffee, then winced when it burned my tongue. "I wanted to talk to him."

"Then go to the police station!"

I tried not to roll my eyes. "I didn't want to have any distractions."

I'd been distracted. So very distracted when I'd been kneeling over his face. Getting him in bed and cuffed to the headboard had been my plan. The orgasm hadn't.

But he'd gotten the point when I'd walked out with his dick hard and his wrists cuffed to his headboard. I knew Claire wasn't his. He knew I was pissed about it. Knew exactly how much. It was supposed to have made me feel better, to give him the proverbial middle finger once and for all.

That hadn't worked out so well, because it was obvious he wanted me. The way he'd looked at me, almost reverently, had been a surprise. The way he'd touched me made me feel sacred. The way he'd practically devoured my pussy, it had seemed as if he truly desired me. To see to my pleasure.

Like it had been all those years ago.

The only truth I knew was on that piece of paper I'd slapped on his rock-hard, bare chest.

Claire wasn't his.

His hard dick? He was just a man, and I'd been a woman in lace.

"What the hell do you have to talk to him about?"

I flicked a glance at my dad but stayed silent. No way did he have a right to details of my private life.

He sighed, held up a hand. "Fine. Don't tell me."

Nothing like a guilt trip.

"I know how you feel about Huck," I said pointedly. "You've made it clear for years." Ever since we first started dating when I was eighteen.

He said something under his breath, but I'd cut down the short hallway, done with our little chat.

I pushed some invoices aside on the desk and set my mug down.

"What are you doing here on a Saturday?" he asked, having followed.

I looked up at him, then pointed at the pile of papers he'd left for me. It was all completely unorganized because he knew I'd take care of it. "Payroll."

His brows winged up. "It's not like you to get behind."

I frowned. Another insult. God, I had no idea why I kept working here. I'd been handling his books since eighth grade. I would walk here after school and sit at this desk and do my homework. The piles of paper had been bigger back then, and I'd figured out the accounting and organized his banking. They were literally books back then. Paper ledgers. I'd been the one who'd bought him computer software when I was eighteen. The one who used it. When I'd gone to college, he'd save months of bookkeeping for my return because he didn't like the computer.

It had been the past two years I'd been back that I'd expected a shift. I'd returned a college graduate. A certified accountant. I'd even worked part-time at a repair shop in Bozeman. I'd hoped to spend my days out in the bay, driving the tow truck. Instead I fell into the bookkeeping and accounting business. I continued to work for him and ensured I paid myself for the effort even though I took on my own clients. *Real* clients.

Around here I also tackled customers, at least on the front end. Ordering. Everything that kept the business afloat except the actual repairs.

I could do that too, but Dad had been adamant I keep my hands clean. Literally.

I wanted to take over, but it hadn't happened yet. All of a sudden I was starting to see it probably wasn't going to either. My father wasn't going to change. The way he was *still* talking about Huck proved that.

"Roy didn't show up yesterday," I replied. "You weren't back. Kale Bradford ran his truck off the road. Graham called me, and I towed it in." I thumbed over my shoulder, indicating the back of the shop. "It's in the lot. I call it totaled since the front axle's bent."

"I'd fire Roy if he wasn't so talented beneath the hood. Hard to find someone with that kind of talent."

"I can do that work," I said. Again. My father didn't even seem to care. All he had to do was retire and enjoy his motorcycle and I'd take over.

He waved me off, then left, grumbling some more.

I powered up my computer as I fumed. He hadn't thanked me for doing two people's jobs *and* coming in on a Saturday.

I sat back in my chair, grabbed my coffee. I needed to stand up to my dad, tell him it was time I took over the entire business. Made it mine. Made changes. Made it grow. He'd been stringing me along, and I'd let him.

Maybe it was seeing Huck that had stirred up my mood. Reminded me of what I'd once had. My old dreams. Plans.

Those had died, though, along with the baby Huck and I had made.

I'd punished Huck. But what had it done for me? Had it made my heart hurt any less? The loss smaller? It hadn't done a thing because I hadn't. Huck had made something of himself, but I hadn't. I was behind this stupid desk, and Huck still wasn't mine.

$\mathcal{H}$UCK

SATURDAY NIGHT

"ONE MORE, DADDY. PLEASE?"

Claire was tucked in beneath my arm on the couch, but she began to wiggle, eager for another story. It was eight and her bedtime.

"Done your routine?" I asked even though I knew.

She nodded, her hair damp and brushed. It was the same wheat-blonde color my hair had been at that age. Even though there wasn't a drop of my blood in her, she was mine whether we looked similar or not.

"I bathed, brushed, and we're doing the books. I don't want to go to bed yet. One more."

Our routine was something my mother had invented for me and my brothers when we were little. Bath, brush, books, bed.

Alice had seen to the first two, and Claire had hunted me down with a pile of books tucked under her arm.

"All right," I pretend grumbled. "One more." She pulled her favorite from the stack and held it out. "Do you think the bear ever finds his missing button?" I asked.

She looked up at me and giggled. "You know what happens, Daddy. We've read this one hundreds of times."

"Then why are we reading it again?"

She wiggled some more and settled in closer, then flipped open to the first page. "Because I like to see him talking to the bird. They're best friends like me and Lizzie."

I started the book, but Claire set her hand over the page so I couldn't keep going.

"Daddy, you said you were working on getting me a mommy."

I sighed, stroked her head. Around lunchtime, Kelsey, one of Claire's preschool teachers, had come to the ranch. I hadn't realized it when Thatcher and I had watched Sawyer fireman carry her out of the auditorium, but she'd been the one to buy him. It had also been the woman to knee him in the balls the other day. Sawyer had it bad if he was still into her after recovering with a bag of frozen peas.

I wasn't the one to talk. Not now. Sarah had stripped me down, got my motor running, and left me handcuffed to my bed.

Claire had wanted Kelsey to have bought me instead of my brother, but Sawyer had told her that I'd been bought too. By someone else.

Claire hadn't forgotten that. It seemed being bought meant getting married. Getting a mommy.

I wanted to marry Sarah. I always had. But clearly there was some shit we had to work through.

Thatcher's heavy footsteps came right before the slap of the back screen door. He lived in the converted old barn and came up to the main house often, usually for Alice's cooking. "Hey, Sprout! I came to say good night before I went to work." He moved behind the couch, grabbed Claire under her arms, and tossed her in the air. He owned a bar in town, the Lucky Spur. Since it was Saturday night, it would be busy and he'd work until well after closing.

She laughed and giggled as he carried her to the big armchair and settled in with her on his lap. "Whatcha doin'?" he asked.

"Daddy's working on getting me a mommy."

The book was clearly forgotten.

Thatcher's red brow went up, and he looked over at me. "Is that so? Who's the lucky lady?"

I wanted to give him the middle finger but not in front of Claire.

She shrugged her tiny shoulders. "Don't know. Earlier he told Miss Kelsey and Seesaw he was working on it."

Alice always said little teapots had big handles, and while the saying was ridiculous, Claire heard everything and filed it away. It was tricky now, but when she was a teenager, I knew I was going to be in big trouble.

"Well, I have a feeling Miss Kelsey's around to stay," he told Claire. I had to agree with him. Sawyer was keeping her. "She loved the puppies earlier, remember?"

Her eyes lit up with childish glee. "She did!" Her face morphed into a frown. "But Miss Kelsey's not going to be my mommy. Who's going to be my mommy?"

I gave Claire *the look*. I was not going to tell a five-year-old my plans, not only because she couldn't keep a secret, but because I didn't want her to get too eager for something that might not happen. I hadn't brought any women around the ranch on purpose.

"He's keeping her a secret, I think," Thatcher said, tickling Claire. "I'd say she's got him all tied up." He smirked and I glared at his joke.

"That's silly." She giggled. "Daddy doesn't need to tie anyone up. He's got handcuffs since he's the chief!"

I could feel my cheeks heat. Fuck me, I wasn't going to live the night before down.

Thatcher's lips were twitching as he tried not to laugh.

I'd gotten free of my bed by rolling onto my stomach, gripping the slat, and pulling it loose. I had a sore shoulder and a headboard that looked a mess as a result. After, I'd gone downstairs to get a drink and ran into Thatcher, who'd been raiding the fridge. He'd seen Sarah leave, and I'd had to tell him the fucking mess. After Sawyer being kneed in the nuts and me getting handcuffed to my own bed, I had to wonder if we had to hand over our man cards.

Thatcher had only stopped laughing when I'd punched him in the arm and showed him the paper Sarah had left with me. He knew who Claire's mother was. Knew I wasn't her biological parent.

"Will you tuck me in, Uncle Thatch?" Fortunately Claire's attention was quickly swayed.

He gave her a bounce on his knee. "Sure. Go up and brush your teeth, and I'll be up."

She popped off his lap and stood before him in her pink pajamas, cocked her head, and set her hands on her hips. "I already brushed."

He leaned in and grinned at her. Bopped her on

the nose. "Good girl. I'm going to count, and let's see how fast you can get in bed and under those covers."

She turned and faced the stairs, put one foot in front of the other as if she were ready to start a race, her arms bent. "Ready."

"Go! One, two, three..."

She bolted out of the room, and we could hear her feet pattering along the wood floor.

Thatcher turned my way, his counting stopped. "Did you decide what you're going to do about Sarah?"

I hadn't. I'd spent the entire day debating. "I *want* to toss her over my knee and spank her ass red for pulling shit like that, but it wasn't a stunt."

"To buy you at the auction to get you into bed so she could leave you like that? She was pissed."

"A total understatement," I grumbled.

"How'd she even find out?" he wondered.

"Kale's accident yesterday."

His eyes widened in surprise. "Seriously? I heard he ran off the road because of a fucking cow?"

"Yup."

He shook his head and laughed.

"I called Graham, who was on duty." Thatcher knew what had happened the night before, but he hadn't heard what I'd figured out earlier. "He confirmed it was Sarah who took the call and towed Kale's truck away from the scene. She must've found his paperwork. Kale's the one who got the letter."

Thatcher grabbed a paperweight off the side table and tossed it back and forth between his hands. "I didn't know Sarah was working for her father."

"Last I heard, she was doing his books." It was a small town, and I was the police chief. "Has been ever since she was a kid and got smarter than her old man in math."

"That's probably not hard to do," he said, setting the paperweight down. He stood and ran a hand over his hair. "He's in the bar often. Pays his tab, but it's always pretty hefty."

I didn't like Bill O'Banyon. He was a total asshole. He didn't like me either, and I knew he thought I was an asshole. He'd made that very clear. I was a punk. A little shit who shouldn't even be *looking* at Sarah, let alone dating her.

While I respected the fact that he protected his daughter, he also didn't see her for who she was. He hadn't thought I was good enough for her, that only a guy like Bunky would do. The little fucker had married Sarah's sister, Lynn. It didn't matter to Bill that his son-in-law couldn't keep his dick out of other women or any of the other stupid shit he did. He'd wanted his daughters to have what he didn't. Wealth. Cars. Status. It didn't matter that Lynn was probably miserable or that Sarah didn't want that lifestyle. He didn't give a shit about what she wanted as long as it had a fancy title or wealthy last name.

Sure, he'd paid for her college, but he wasn't rolling in cash like Bunky.

All Sarah had ever wanted was to be a mechanic and run a shop. Just like her dad. She'd once told me that dream, been eager for it. But since the only time I'd heard of Sarah going on a tow recently was for Kale's truck, it was obvious he was stringing her along. Why she hadn't set up her own business since she'd finished college and graduate school, I had no idea. I had to wonder what was keeping her there.

I'd seen her tinker in the past. She knew her shit when it came to engines.

"What's that smile for?" he asked.

"She fixed the fucking tractor when none of us could figure out what was wrong with it."

She'd been eighteen and still in high school.

Thatcher tipped his head back and laughed. "God, I forgot about that."

"Uncle Thatch!" Claire's voice carried from her room.

Thatcher gave a little wave as he left the great room. I couldn't miss his shouting, "I think that was seventeen seconds. The fastest yet."

I loved that my brother tucked Claire in, that they were close. Alice was there for her for any girl-type things that came up, but thankfully there weren't too many at this age. But Alice was ready to move and be near her sister in Alabama. Claire needed a mother, and the only woman I'd ever pictured for the job had been Sarah. But I'd assumed Claire would be a baby we made together. That she'd be the one tucking my daughter in. I'd also assumed we'd live happily ever after.

That hadn't turned out. But Sarah's actions the night before had changed everything. She was pissed at me. She was still hot for me. I could still taste her sticky honey on my tongue. I'd been given a second chance with her. Sarah might not know it, but she'd set the two of us back in motion. She was going to be mine again.

$\mathcal{H}$UCK

*S*ATURDAY NIGHT

I COULD HEAR the music from the street. People spilled out of the Lucky Spur's entrance, a fun weekend night in The Bend. Thatcher had converted an old mill into a bar. It was cavernous and brick. One large room with concrete floors. A large patio area that was on the river, fairy lights strung overhead to brighten the space. Large garage doors lined the one wall to the outdoor seating and were all open.

I wasn't here to drink even though I was off shift.

Thatcher had called me around eleven to give me the heads-up that Sarah was here. With a man.

No fucking way was that okay. I'd made her come the night before. In my bed. Even if she was angry with me, that pussy was mine.

I took off my Stetson when I entered, went to the bar, and waited to catch Thatcher's eye. He came down the line with two drinks, handed them off to a woman along with a wink. When he got to me, he tipped his head toward the back.

I looked in that direction, and there she was. With a fucking guy. I didn't care if he was helping her with a Sunday School program for church.

Just seeing Sarah across a crowded room made my dick hard. My mouth watered for another taste of her. She might have been trying to punish me, but all it had done was make me want her more. Since she was here with someone, it was my turn to be angry.

I remembered how she used to respond to me all those years ago. Melting beneath my kiss, whimpering beneath my touch. But now? She was heat and fire. Passionate and wild. And she'd given all of that to me.

When she'd slapped the paper on my chest, I'd seen her anger. Fuck, how could I have missed it? I'd also seen her heat.

I sidled up to her high top. She and her *friend* looked up at me. The guy stared wide-eyed in my direction.

"Huck," Sarah said, swallowing hard. "I was just—"

"Leaving," I finished for her, standing beside their table, feet spread wide.

"Sarah, you know him?" the guy asked, then swallowed hard. Good, he was afraid of me. He should be for even looking her way.

"I know you," I said, setting my hands on my hips. "Two reckless driving citations and a night in jail for drunk and disorderly."

The guy—Brad Blaison—flushed. Yeah, I had the right guy. He wasn't a total fuckup, but he didn't deserve to even look at Sarah.

"Find another target, Brad," I told him.

He hopped up faster than the Easter Bunny and disappeared into the crowd.

Sarah stood as well. For one so small, she had a lot of fury. "You're an asshole."

I didn't move. "I've heard that before."

She rolled her eyes and looked away, then headed for the entrance. Since it was the direction I wanted her to go, I didn't say a word, only followed.

Once we were outside, I set my hat back on my head, then reached out and grabbed Sarah's hand. "Where are you taking me?" she asked.

I didn't say anything, just led her to my truck. I'd parked far from the entrance, near the road. Out of habit, I'd backed into the spot. There was an empty space next to my truck.

"You want a guy, baby girl, I'm right here."

"Stop calling me that," she snapped, running a hand through her hair. It was wild and long down her back. She had on another dress, this one missing the damned tie at the hip. It was yellow and had a little ruffle just above the knee. The neckline dipped in a V that all but invited my hand to slip into it and cup her small breast. Brush the nipple with my thumb.

I'd always called her *baby girl*. She was six years younger than me and had been eighteen when we first got together. While I wasn't into being her daddy, I'd always want to take care of her. Protect her. Based on how I'd reacted when she was sitting inside with Brad, I was still pretty fucking possessive, too.

She turned and faced away from me. I could see the roll of her shoulders, the way she was looking down at the ground. "As for being my guy, you lost that chance a long time ago."

"And I got it back last night when you sat on my face."

"How dare you!" It was pretty dark, but I was sure her cheeks were a bright pink when she spun back.

"You pressed your knees into my ears all on your own. I didn't force you since I was cuffed to the fucking headboard."

If looks could kill, I'd be dead on the ground. "I can't believe you said that!"

"No more Brads," I warned.

She set her hands on her slim hips. "For your information, I came here with my friend Jane. Brad stopped by, asking after work for my dad."

Stopped by? He hadn't left since Thatcher had called me. I lifted my chin. "Text Jane and let her know you're with me and not coming back."

Her mouth dropped open and she sputtered. "I'm not going *anywhere* with you."

"Maybe not, but you're done in there." I leaned back against my truck and crossed my arms. She could argue all she wanted. She wasn't going back inside. Brad may have wanted an *interview*, but no one did that at a bar on a Saturday night. He'd wanted a different kind of job, one that involved getting under her pretty yellow dress.

Muttering, she grabbed her cell from the purse she had slung over her shoulder and sent the message. Shoved the phone away.

"There, satisfied?"

Slowly I shook my head. "Not yet. Not until you are. I might have gotten you off last night, but it was clear afterward that you sure as fuck weren't happy."

Her hands fell to her sides. "Huck."

"You got questions for me. Ask. You don't need to handcuff me to do that."

"Why didn't you tell me Claire wasn't yours?" She snapped her mouth shut as if the words had fallen out by accident.

"She's mine."

"Not biologically," she countered, shaking her head. Her blonde hair flew around her shoulders as she did so.

"The way that matters the least." Once I'd learned the truth, Mandy had admitted she had no idea who Claire's actual father was. She'd said it could have been a number of guys, but not me.

It was one thing on a long list I'd shared with Kale in case Mandy ever came back to try to claim custody. Which it seemed she had.

"A sperm donor doesn't make a guy a good father."

"I thought..." She cut off, set her fingers over her lips. She wasn't angry now. She seemed upset. Sad.

"What? What did you think?"

"That you'd moved on to someone else right after me."

I'd broken it off with her at the end of July, not long before she headed to Bozeman. I'd left for Helena directly after. Claire had been born the following May. If someone took the time to do the math, which Sarah obviously had, she was right. I'd have gone from taking her virginity in the back of my pickup, the same one I leaned against, to Mandy's bed within a few weeks.

Except I'd never been in Mandy's bed.

I pushed off the truck. Shrugged. "You believed the same as everyone else."

"Believed—" She sputtered, stared at me. "Are you

kidding me? You came home with a baby! Why would you have an infant that's not yours?"

I pointed at her. "That. Right there. You think I gave a shit then what people thought of me? Or now?"

"I thought you cared about what *I* thought."

"I did." I ran a hand over my face.

She huffed out a laugh. "You have a funny way of showing it."

I sighed. "You found out Claire's not my biological child. She's legally mine though. I'm her daddy, and that's all that matters. All she'll ever know."

I laced that with a hint of warning in case she had any ridiculous ideas.

"You walked away from me. Told me you were holding me back. You had no job besides working the ranch. The town knew you as a slacker."

"Your father's word, I believe," I countered.

Tears welled in her eyes. "I tried, Huck. Tried to change your mind. I wanted you just as you were. God, I loved you."

That hit my chest harder than any bullet.

"If I'd known the truth about the baby, it would have been different."

I shook my head. "And yet I stopped being a slacker and got my shit together. You didn't come to me until last night."

She stared at me. I doubt she even blinked. I hadn't been able to tell her the truth. I'd walked so her family didn't get ripped to shreds back then, and it wouldn't make a difference now.

"What I want to know is when you'll be in my bed again." She wasn't the only one who wanted answers. "This time to stay."

Her mouth dropped open. Then closed. Then open again. "I don't want that!"

I smirked. "Really? Your nipples and dripping pussy last night said otherwise."

"How dare you!"

"You're the one that bought me, baby girl. For five hundred dollars, you at least deserve a little dick, don't you think?"

She came over and slapped me across the face. It rocked my head to the side and stung like a bitch, but I'd made my point.

I took hold of her shoulders and pulled her close. "Why are you so outraged? Because your plan backfired? You wanted to get back at me for keeping the secret about Claire, but you discovered you still have feelings for me."

"Feelings of hatred."

"And lust. You want me."

"God, how does your ego fit in your truck with you?"

"If you didn't want me, you wouldn't have climbed into my bed. Knelt over my face."

"Women can only get off if their feelings are involved?" she countered.

"I don't give a shit about other women. I care about you. *You* can't. You're a one-man woman, baby girl."

"You think that man's you?"

"It always was. I just had to make something of myself. Make myself worthy."

"Like I said, I loved you just the way you were. You didn't have to prove anything to me."

I shook my head. "Your father was right. But I got my shit together. Graduated the academy, became a deputy."

She held up a hand. "Wait. What does my father have to do with this?"

"He's always hated me. You knew that." I shrugged, remembering his harsh words. "I proved him wrong. Then *you* proved me wrong when you didn't come to me after that first year of school."

"You keep saying this. There was *no* way I'd come back to you after what you did. What I *thought* you did." She set her hand on my chest, tipped her chin up, and blinked. "Why do I have to repeat myself? I thought you'd been with someone else, wanted her enough to make a child." She wilted then, as if she'd been deflated like a balloon.

"Claire's mine. How that came to be doesn't matter."

"It does to me!" She sighed, blinked hard as if

willing tears back. "It took me a long time to get over you, Huck. I can't go through that again." She looked down at the ground.

I remembered that time like it was yesterday. Sarah and I had spent the night together in the back of my pickup. I'd driven us onto the back forty on the ranch by a creek. I'd packed a late-night picnic and made a bed of old blankets. She'd given herself to me that night. It had been perfect. Hot as fuck. Sarah had been sweet in her innocence. Sexy.

A few days later her father had met me at the door. Told me to call it off. Threatened Sarah's college chances. So I'd walked.

That had been my wake-up call. The one thing that I wanted, I wasn't worthy of. So I'd tried to make myself worthy of her. I'd made something of myself so she could be proud of me. So my parents would have as well. I'd even saved an infant from a fucked-up life. One look at the tiny, squirming blonde bundle and I'd known it was going to be me. I'd just hoped it would also be Sarah.

I squeezed her shoulders. "So last night. Why'd you do it?"

"I found that paper in Kale's truck. Seeing it and learning the truth? I was so angry. All those years ago you made me think—"

"I didn't make you think anything," I countered. "You did it all by yourself. With your daddy's help."

"Don't bring him into this."

I agreed with her. Bill had pulled us apart before. I was thirty-fucking-two years old. I didn't need to go through Sarah's daddy to be with her any longer.

Pulling her into me, I leaned down and kissed her. I couldn't be gentle, not now, not when I was desperate for her. My frustration and need, my longing and craving for this woman poured out of my kiss. I licked into her, remembered her taste. I tangled my fingers in her hair, and I angled her head as I wanted. I knew the second she gave over, her body all but melting into mine. I wrapped an arm around her to hold her up, pressed her curves into me.

"Fuck, baby girl, you're so sweet," I murmured in her ear right before I nipped it. Then I went back to her mouth. Feasting. Plunging. Consuming. I turned us and backed her into the side of my truck, and let my knee wedge between hers, and she began to ride my thigh.

I had no idea how long it went on for, but when my hand was up her dress and playing with the lacy edge of her panties, I remembered we were in a fucking parking lot.

I settled my forehead against hers.

"It's just you and me, baby girl. Always has been."

"Huck," she whispered, licking her swollen lips.

"I think it's time you had a little chat with your daddy."

I could understand him wanting to protect his daughter. Hell, I'd probably do the same for Claire when she was eighteen and a guy was sniffing around her. I'd even have my service pistol out when I did it.

But I'd walked away just like he'd wanted. I hadn't done it for him but for Sarah. Then I put myself on the path to make her mine by going to the academy, and it had all fallen to shit. I wouldn't trade Claire for anything, but I'd always had what-ifs. I did now, especially with her in my arms.

Sarah wasn't a kid any longer. She was a grown woman and knew the truth.

She shook her head. "You're the one that walked. Who never believed in us. That I'd go to school and then run my own shop. That you'd be there for me."

I stepped back, ran my hand over my mouth. It didn't erase her taste. My dick was still punching against the front of my jeans to get out. "Oh yeah? I always believed in you. That's why I left. So I wouldn't hold you back. But who's holding stopping you now? If your daddy believes in you, then why aren't you running the shop? Why doesn't he let you work on the cars? Every time I'm on a scene with Roy, he's nothing but a lazy ass. Your father would rather employ that fucker than you, his own daughter."

A gasp escaped her lips, and she bumped my shoulder to get away. She ran across the lot. No question she hated my guts now.

I stepped out into the middle of the lot and watched her head to her car. That was no fucking car. It was a vintage Jeep Wagoneer in mint condition. No doubt she'd overhauled the engine and done all the work herself.

"That went fucking well," I muttered after her brake lights disappeared out of the lot. I climbed back into my truck. I had to shift in my seat to get comfortable, my dick as hard as it had ever been.

9

ARAH

Sunday, 4 a.m.

I WANTED to take over O'Banyons, but this was one part of the job I hated. Four a.m. was not my favorite time of day. I'd been tossing and turning for a second night in a row, thinking of Huck. Of what he'd said. Of my life and what I'd done with it. Or hadn't done. The fight. The kiss. *Oh, the kiss.* He was right. I felt things for him. Enough to make out with him in the Lucky Spur's parking lot. It had made me wet, horny, and definitely cranky.

I must have fallen asleep, because my cell had woken me.

Graham had called for the second time for a tow. I mentally cursed Roy for being a drunk, lazy ass and my father for enabling the guy. Where the hell were those two? If I wasn't supposed to be doing anything but the books behind a desk, then why weren't they answering their damned phones?

I'd thrown on some clothes and driven to the shop to pick up the tow truck, wondering if I was enabling them as well. I was a doormat to them. They assumed I'd take care of everything. Clean up all the messes. Fill in for them when they decided to be lazy, drunk, entitled jerks.

I had. Blindly. For *years*. God, I'd been doing my dad's accounting for even longer than that. He'd forgotten how to do it. I was starting to see nothing would change unless I did.

I cut through the early morning darkness on the way out of town, riding high in the tow truck. The seat was old and had me bouncing over the slightest bump.

I'd been back from Bozeman for two years. In that time I'd built up my accounting business. Had good local clients. But I'd gotten nowhere with my dad. The one person who should've been helping me fulfill my dreams. He knew I wanted to run the shop. I'd made it clear over and over.

And yet he stalled, just like a car with water in the gas tank.

I eased off the accelerator as the flashing blue and red lights came into view. I was on the two-lane stretch that connected The Bend to the interstate. It was a straight and level road, but accidents happened. I flipped on my hazards and the yellow tow lights on the roof and slowed to a crawl as I took in the scene that was well lit from a fire truck and two police cars. I counted six first responders milling around.

There was a single car off the road. Flipped. I pulled past the scene, then parked on the shoulder. Cutting the engine, I hopped down from the cab, grabbed the reflective vest that was tucked into the pocket on the door, and shrugged it on. Then I grabbed my leather gloves.

I walked around the back and down into the ditch. The four-door sedan was snagged on the barbed-wire fence that ran along the road. The car was set back about fifteen feet, and from the wheel tracks that cut through the mud and grass, it must've been going pretty fast.

I had to figure out how best to get the tow truck into place so I could use the winch to get the vehicle up onto the bed. Since it was upside down, front or back didn't matter.

I pushed up the slight incline and came into the beam of the fire truck's bright lights. I raised my foot to step, but freaked and jumped back, practically high stepping like a horse. It wasn't a snake, which usually made me lose my shit. But this was no snake. There on the ground was a body. A very dead one based on the fact his head was turned at an angle only seen in exorcisms from '80s horror movies. It was the fence post that stuck through his chest that made bile rise in my throat. A strange gasp escaped, and I felt the blood rush from my face and my fingers began to tingle.

I hadn't seen the body and almost stepped on it...

I stared and stared. Sweat dotted my forehead, and I wasn't sure if I wanted to vomit or bolt. I'd never seen a dead body before, not even at a wake all dressed and peaceful.

This guy had died violently, clearly flung from the car when it had either flipped or made impact with the ground after.

"What the hell are you doing here?"

I jumped and spun around at the rough voice. The same one who'd scolded me earlier at the bar. Huck. He loomed over me, half of him caught in deep shadow so he looked ominous.

I almost stumbled on the uneven ground, but his hand on my elbow kept me steady, then pulled me away from the body.

How was it I'd made it six years barely seeing the guy and now I couldn't stop running into him? His touch was reassuring. Steadying.

I swallowed hard, bile in my throat. "I... I got called to tow a car."

He finally stopped when we were back on the side of the road, lit by headlights from one of the police cars. He ran a hand over his face, then set it on the hilt of his weapon at his hip. He had on his Stetson and jeans but looked official in his uniform shirt with the shiny star on the chest and utility belt. He hadn't been wearing it earlier at the Lucky Spur. I had no idea why I thought of that now.

If his weary eyes were any indicator, he hadn't slept all that much either. But they were sharp, narrowed. His jaw was clenched and covered in whiskers. Even lit up by the harsh red and blue lights, I couldn't miss that he was pissed.

He glanced over his shoulder. "Where the hell is Roy?"

I didn't answer his question, only blinked at him, then shivered. "That guy... God, Huck, that guy—"

I was yanked against Huck's solid chest, and his arms went around me. One big hand slid up and down my back. The other cupped my head. My cheek was pressed into his uniform shirt, and I started to cry.

It was because a guy had died in a car accident, definitely. But Huck was holding me, giving me comfort. I'd relied on him to protect me when we'd dated, and I'd loved it. Craved the way I'd felt safe. I'd forgotten what his hugs were like. How he smelled. In the fresh night air I breathed in his scent. Rugged and dark. Laundry detergent but also man. He was warm and steady, powerful and protective.

"I'm sorry you saw that, baby girl," he murmured, then kissed my hair. "Just take a minute."

I nodded against his chest and slowly pulled myself together. I should be hating him after what he'd said earlier, but I couldn't. Not now.

With a gentle tug on my hair, he tipped my head back so I had to look up at him. "Where the hell is Roy?"

I stiffened at the repeated question, then frowned. "Why does everyone think I can't do this? I know I'm small, but I'm not lifting the car onto the tow truck."

"You should be safe in bed, not out here. Where's Roy?"

He wasn't going to settle until he got his answer.

"He didn't answer his cell, I guess. Graham called me."

"Graham has your number?" If Huck had fur, he'd have a stripe raised up his back based on the way he asked.

I rolled my eyes. "Yes, Graham and I are having a wild fling. He calls me to meet him. At car accidents. It's pretty hot."

"Talk like that gets you over my knee, baby girl."

I wasn't sure if I wanted to punch him in the throat or climb him like a tree for that. The one time we'd had sex, it had been hot. A little frantic, but I'd been a virgin and had had no clue what I was doing. It had hurt like hell, too, even though Huck had been gentle.

But I'd learned I didn't want gentle. He'd been holding back with me, and for my first time I was thankful. But I wasn't a virgin any longer, and my needs weren't tame. Or at least they weren't tame with Huck.

I *wanted* him to take me over his knee. Then fuck me hard.

That wasn't what I needed to think about right now. Or ever. I stepped back from his hold. Remembered where I was. That it was Huck standing in front of me. I shouldn't be seeking comfort from him. I hated him. Right?

"Then stop asking stupid questions," I snapped.

His lips thinned, and his gaze shifted between mine. I felt as if I was a suspect and he was waiting for me to admit my guilt to a crime.

"Head back to your truck. It's going to take a little time. The preschool downtown, Claire's preschool, was set on fire earlier. An eyewitness put this car"—he tipped his head toward the flipped vehicle—"at the scene. There's a gas can and other evidence that has to be gone through."

"God, was anyone hurt?"

He shook his head, but his jaw clenched tight. I was sure he was thinking about his daughter and the other children being caught in a fire. Some of my fight left me then, realizing all that Huck had stacked on his shoulders.

"Someone will get you when it's time to load the car." He turned, then shifted back. Lowered his head before I could even blink, and kissed me hard and fast. His mouth was firm, intent. His tongue plundered for one delicious lick. Then he stalked off.

"That's it?" I called, setting my fingers on my lips. "Wait?"

He stopped, looked over his shoulder at me. "You need to talk to your daddy."

$\mathcal{H}$ UCK

I PULLED my police SUV up in front of the main house. Kelsey climbed out and didn't look back, meeting Alice on the front porch. The older woman put her arms around Kelsey's shoulders and led her inside. Kelsey hated me because I'd arrested her so she'd be forced to talk to Sawyer. It was complicated and their own story, but yeah, she wasn't happy with me. That was fine. What was important was that she loved Sawyer, even when he was hotheaded.

It had been a clusterfuck at the station after we got back from the rollover. Since Kelsey had been the only witness to the fire the night before, Sawyer had brought her in to write a statement. Bunky, a guy we'd grown up with who was a total asshole, had shown up for a report to file with insurance because he was the owner of the preschool building that had burned. But it turned out he was also Kelsey's ex. She'd followed him to Montana and found out he was a lying douche canoe and was married—to Sarah's sister, Lynn—and had two kids. In the station lobby, Sawyer had punched Bunky in the face for being an asshole to Kelsey and had stormed off, pissed.

There were details I didn't know, but I'd driven Kelsey to the ranch because she had no place to go since it turned out she'd been living in the preschool that burned. I had a feeling that once Sawyer cooled off, he'd be thankful she was safe. And here on the ranch where she belonged. He loved her. That was obvious. That was why I got involved, even if it had Kelsey hating my guts.

She had to wait her turn, because Sarah was at the front of the line for that.

I loved Sarah. Always had. I'd only pushed the idea of it down deep so I didn't have to feel how much it hurt to crave someone I couldn't have. Bill O'Banyon had seen to that. Claire's birth had put the nail in the coffin of our relationship.

But Sawyer was whipped. Ever since Kelsey had kneed him in the balls, from what I'd figured.

But *Bunky*? That was a fucking bump in the road Sawyer was going to have to get over. I huffed out a laugh, because fortunately for me, I never had to worry about Sarah getting together with her brother-in-law.

At least one of the O'Banyon daughters had done what Daddy wanted and married well. But Lynn wasn't the sister I cared about.

I pulled around the circle driveway and back down the lane to the main road. I'd been up all night. Based on Kelsey's account, it appeared the dead guy was the suspected arsonist. He wasn't going to be setting any more fires, but it was going to be hard to figure out *why* he'd set this one in the first place with him in the morgue.

All I wanted to do was climb into bed and sleep the day away, but that wasn't going to happen. I had so much fucking paperwork from the two calls I'd be lucky if I got home by dinner.

My cell rang, and since I was driving, I didn't check the display. I pushed the button to answer through speaker mode.

"Manning."

"Ignoring me and my lawyer isn't going to make me go away."

The cranky voice had me grimacing. *Fuck.* Mandy.

I'd meant to call her after talking with Kale in the ER, and deal with her shit, but I'd gotten sidetracked.

"I have a job, unlike you," I said. I didn't know if that was the case, but it was a pretty good guess.

"I'm filing for custody."

"Why? You haven't given a shit before now." I wasn't even sure why I was wasting my breath. I should let Kale deal with her and keep me from stroking out.

"Because she's my daughter."

"Bullshit. You haven't called, sent cards, presents. Nothing. You don't give a shit about her. What's the real reason?"

She stayed silent.

"You want more money."

"I'm her mother!" Her voice was shrill and agitated.

"And that makes you deserving of compensation?"

"Yes," she replied. "I *made* her."

I shook my head, pushed the button to lower the window so the fresh air came in. Made Claire? I thought of Maple and her puppies.

I counted to ten, then gritted out, "You do realize extorting a cop isn't the smartest of ideas."

"I want custody. I'll petition for it."

"Bullshit," I said again. I'd initially paid her so she'd go away. She didn't want Claire, but she'd put me on the birth certificate and told me Claire was mine because she knew I had deep pockets. Eighteen years' worth. But when I'd learned the truth, having my name as Claire's legal father had screwed her over. She hadn't been able to put Claire up for adoption without my consent.

The only thing she could do was walk. And the fifty grand incentive I'd given her to do so had worked. But now she was back for more.

"It's been five years, Mandy. Why the fuck are you back now? The cash didn't hold you?"

"I have bills."

Bills. More like she owed someone. Drugs. Gambling. Whatever.

I'd pay her. Hell, I'd sell the ranch if it meant keeping Claire safe. But Mandy was stupid. A judge would see through her petition. Through everything. Eventually. She'd drag this shit out if it meant a chance at some cash. She wasn't stupid. She knew I was protective of Claire and was extorting that, too.

Fuck me.

I finally had a chance with Sarah, and Mandy was back.

I wanted a life with Sarah. I wanted her to know Claire, to be her mother. They hadn't even met and the image was so perfect it made my breath catch. But having Mandy in the picture, fucking with all that, was not okay. I'd dealt with Mandy because I'd made her my business. But Sarah didn't owe the woman anything. She deserved a family. Peace. Not a greedy drug addict threatening to destroy it all.

It was time to wean Mandy off the money tit. To make her gone for good. Because with her around, I couldn't be completely free to have Sarah. The fact that Sarah had handcuffed me to my bed proved that.

"Try your shit if you want, but know this. You're not getting near Claire. She's not what you want. You don't give a shit about her. Didn't even ask how she was, what she looks like. I'll get to the point. You're not getting shit from me. Not one dime."

"You're a Manning. You've got more money than you can spend."

"I do," I said. "I'll spend all of it to see you fail. Like I said. Go back under the rock you crawled out from under because I'm not your sugar daddy."

"You're an asshole," she shouted.

I sighed. "So I've been told."

I hung up. There was nothing new to say, and all talking would do was piss me off further. And her. The way she'd gotten more and more wound up as we spoke definitely meant she was unstable. I wanted her nowhere near me. Nowhere near Claire. I'd get Kale on it once he was off the pain pills, make her go away for good, because if I did it, she'd be buried in the back forty somewhere.

I didn't hurt women, but Mandy? I'd make an exception because she was using my five-year-old as a pawn.

I thought of Sarah, of what kind of mother she'd

be. How sweet she was—except right now with me—and caring. Thoughtful. Kind. Gentle. Hot as fuck. Passionate.

Shit. I thought of her riding my face. The only sweet she'd been then was sweet *tasting*.

If we hadn't broken up, she'd have my ring on her finger and a few kids by now. I could imagine her belly round with my child.

My dick hardened at the idea of filling her with my cum and knocking her up. We'd have a little girl that had her fair hair. A few boys, too, to protect her. A brood of them.

But then I wouldn't have Claire, who was too precious to me to consider what-ifs. She was mine, and I wouldn't change a thing. But for some reason I'd been given a second chance with Sarah. Sure, it was totally fucked up. She hadn't approached me because she wanted me back, but because she'd been pissed off.

I huffed out a laugh and turned onto the main road. The Manning boys sure knew how to pick 'em. Kelsey was a red-haired spitfire with a hellish temper. I'd laughed at Sawyer when he told us how she'd kneed him in the balls. I could only imagine how he'd laugh right back after he learned how I'd had to break my headboard to get free of what Sarah had done.

"Chief, we have a 10-16 in progress." The voice through the radio was the daytime station manager. She'd been at the job for decades, knew the town inside and out. Knew the people in it in more detail than any gossiping busybody.

With one hand on the steering wheel, I ran the other over my face again.

"There a reason you're telling me specifically about a domestic dispute, Noreen?" She could've sent any of the deputies on duty. Unless Bunky was still at the station filling out the police report for the fire, then Graham was most likely free.

"Affirmative, Chief. O'Banyons Auto Shop. Someone was walking by and heard shouting. Figured you might want to check it out."

The location perked me up better than any cup of coffee. She knew my history with Sarah. Knew she'd bought me at the auction. I doubted Noreen had any idea I'd been handcuffed to my bed, but I wouldn't be surprised if she did.

I appreciated her letting me know. I had a feeling Sarah had finally had that chat with her daddy. And that she'd had enough. If someone called it in, it had to be pretty heated. Sarah had stood up to me the other night, but I wasn't sure how she'd do with Bill. Which meant it was finally time for me to step in.

"Copy that. On my way."

$\mathcal{S}$ARAH

"WHY ARE you so angry about me going to the accident?" I asked my dad, pretty upset myself. "You didn't answer Graham's call and neither did Roy."

I'd finally gotten the totaled car off-loaded to the lot behind the shop, and I needed an IV of coffee. When Dad came in, I'd been in the service bay washing my hands at the industrial sink. He went over to the wall and slapped the button that opened one of the garage doors. It rose with a loud whir. The breeze came in and made my hair blow into my face. He was stalling.

"Where *were* you?" I asked. "And is Roy even alive?"

After seeing the dead body earlier, I shouldn't have asked the question, but really, where was the guy?

I'd sat in the cab until about six, dozing on and off, before I could winch the car out of the ditch. The sun had just peeked over the horizon. The coroner had come and gone by then, along with the dead body. I wasn't going to forget that sight for a long time. From what Huck had said, it was assumed the driver had been the one to start the fire at the preschool. No one had been hurt, but the building was pretty damaged. A witness had seen him flee in the car that was flipped. By the scent of liquor wafting from the interior, he'd had too much to drink and got himself killed.

"I'm angry because I don't want you going on calls," he snapped. "How many times do I have to tell you the same thing?"

I was exhausted. Riled. Confused. Ever since I'd found out about Huck and Claire Manning, I'd been completely out of whack. My average, boring life had somehow changed. I saw things I hadn't noticed before.

One became very obvious. He was stringing me along. "You're never going to give me the shop, are you?" I asked, setting my damp hands on my hips.

It had been my assumption that I'd take over from him. He'd taught me the foundation for all I knew about fixing a car; then continued those skills in Bozeman while in college. I knew engines. I did the books. The ordering. I could handle the tow truck. I could do it all probably better than my dad. Hell, *he couldn't do it without me.*

"Why can't you be like your sister?" he shouted, glaring.

I crossed my arms over my chest, leaned against the sink. "You want me to marry an asshole who isn't faithful?"

"This life isn't for you." He waved his arm through the air, indicating the shop where three cars sat waiting to be worked on.

"Why not? Because I should marry a guy with money? Who plays golf and gets me a fancy car?"

"Yes!"

"You think Lynn is happy?"

"Of course she's happy," he snapped back. His dark eyes sparked with anger, completely irrational in his thinking.

"Bunky can't keep it in his pants, Dad," I said. How did he not know that? "Why would you want a guy like that for me?"

The idea was insulting.

I thought of Huck. I'd assumed he'd dumped me and moved on to another woman within a month. That was the reason I'd never gone back to him. Never even approached him to ask what had happened. He'd had a baby. I'd thought he hadn't been able to keep it in his pants like Bunky.

I'd thought about calling Huck so many times. Had typed his number in, then deleted it. But I wasn't going to be unhappy like Lynn.

I had standards that obviously my dad didn't even care about. I wanted a solid relationship. One built on trust. On love. I'd thought I had that with Huck. But then everything I believed had been wrong.

"I'm right, aren't I?" I tucked my hair back behind my ear again. Even though it was pulled back in a sloppy ponytail, long strands had come free, and the summer breeze swirled through the open bay. Fresh air cut the tang of oil and metal. "You're not going to give me the shop."

He pointed to himself in his Harley T-shirt and old jeans. There was a stain on the denim and a slight tear at the hem of the shirt. "Do I look like I'm old enough to retire?"

"You're old enough to know that Roy is a deadbeat and that your own daughter does his job and all the bookkeeping. And yours sometimes too."

He ignored my words. "You don't know what you want."

I stared at him, wide-eyed. "I'm twenty-six years old! You don't get to decide for me."

"Like you make the best choices. You were going down the wrong path. You're doing it again. Friday night proves it."

I stilled. My heart kicked up a notch. "The auction. You mean Huck Manning."

"Yes."

"You didn't answer my question."

"About what? Manning? I told you he wasn't good enough for you."

"I mean about taking over O'Banyons."

He took a step closer and used his height to his advantage. I never thought he'd hurt me physically, but he was playing games with me. Trying to intimidate me and keep me cowered. Like I had been ever since I'd returned from school.

He stared me down, and I refused to be the first who looked away. "No. I won't have you taking it over."

Even though I'd figured the truth, the words hurt. The finality of it. The proof of what I'd been suspecting. I took a deep breath, tried to will back the tears. The last thing I wanted was for him to see how much he'd hurt me. "So you were going to, what, just use me?"

He frowned. He actually looked confused. "Use you? You pay yourself, don't you?"

I looked at my father, the man I'd wanted to emulate ever since I was little.

"Why'd you show me how to fix cars if you never wanted me to do it?" Yeah, the tears were winning, and they clogged my throat.

He shrugged. "It was cheaper than a babysitter. I had work to do, and I couldn't just leave you at home."

Wow. Holy fuck.

I tossed the paper towel in the barrel trash can, then threw up my hands. "I'm out. Find yourself a new Girl Friday."

"What the fuck's a Girl Friday?" he shouted. "Pumpkin, I don't know what's gotten into you."

It wasn't Huck Manning, that was for sure. My pussy clenched with a need for him. I remembered how he'd held me earlier in the darkness. How he'd kissed me in the bar's parking lot. How he'd made me come all over his face.

He'd *saved* a baby from a bad situation. He gave and gave while people like my dad thought shit about him.

Maybe I had too.

"I'll make it clearer for you. I quit."

I cut down the space between one of the cars and the wall. My dad stepped into my path, blocking my exit. I looked up at him, tipped my chin, defiant.

"What are you going to do?" he asked as if I was nothing without him. Like I would be out on the street if I didn't stick around.

"Run my own shop." I'd said it. Said my dream aloud. It was time to make it happen.

He laughed, set his hands on his hips. "Right."

Disbelief laced that one word. He had zero faith. He didn't believe in me or anything I did.

"A stupid decision just like you buying Manning the other night. What is it, that time of the month?"

God, my father was an asshole! What had Huck told me? That my father had some explaining to do?

The only story I knew was that Huck hadn't wanted me and then came home with a baby. A baby I'd thought he'd made after tossing me aside.

But that wasn't true. I knew now that Huck hadn't broken up with me and moved on. If I took Claire out of the picture, it was much clearer.

What was the truth? We'd been in love, made plans. I'd given him my virginity, which he'd said made me his. Then he'd come to the house. Broke up with me. My dad had been there. Observing it all.

"What did you do?" I asked. "All those years ago. With Huck Manning."

The corner of his mouth tipped up. "He wasn't good enough for you."

"Yeah, you've always said that."

"I told him he was holding you back."

I frowned. "When?"

He gave a small shrug as if it didn't mean anything to him. "Before you went to school."

"Why would you do that?"

"You were headed to college. He could offer you nothing."

He'd given me his love. His protection. His promises that he'd keep me safe. Keep me happy.

"He's not nothing, Dad. He's the chief of police! I'd say he's made a man of himself."

"He had a baby with another woman right after he dumped you."

I knew the truth of that now. He hadn't. Huck was right, people in this town were going to judge no matter what had actually happened, and I had no intention of setting my dad straight.

"I'm not talking about then. I'm talking before I left for school. He came and said he was breaking up with me because of school. Because he was bad for me. Why would he all of a sudden say that?"

"Because I told him the truth."

My dad had talked to Huck. "What did you say?" My throat ached, trying to ask the question.

Dad shrugged. "That he needed to leave you alone or I'd step in."

"That wasn't stepping in?" I shouted. I pushed at his chest, and he stepped back, more out of surprise than because of my strength. "You drove him away!"

"I did it for you."

"I know Huck. We were in love. He would have fought for me. He'd have taken me away."

He didn't say anything, but he wasn't bending in his thoughts toward Huck Manning.

"You threatened him." He was stone-faced. "Oh my God. What did you do?"

"I told him I wasn't going to put you through college. That I'd take all the money away."

I'd had a scholarship, but it had been a partial one. My dad had told me he'd pay for the rest of tuition and room and board, and I'd been thankful for that. Maybe that was why I'd stuck around all these years helping him, as if I owed him or felt indebted.

But it had all been a lie.

"I did it for you, pumpkin."

"You didn't do it for me. You did it because you hate Huck Manning. I have no idea what he did or why, but he's not what you think. He never was." Tears slid down my cheeks.

I turned away, felt sick. Six years. *Six years* and I never knew the truth. "All this time, I thought he hated me. That I wasn't special enough. Good enough. That what we'd shared had been a lie."

That he'd taken my virginity as a feat to achieve instead of something special. A beginning for us.

I thought of the baby we'd made that night. When I'd learned I was pregnant, I was already at school. Huck had been gone. The baby was a culmination of our love, but it hadn't been real. For a bit I'd hated the baby I'd carried because it was a reminder of the lie of our relationship.

When I'd lost it... I'd thought it was meant to be. I

hadn't been worthy of being a mother. Since our relationship was dead, so was any proof of it.

He'd walked away for me.

"So? Like I said, not even a year later he came back with another woman's baby. Proof I was right."

The only thing it proved was how wrong my dad had been. Huck was a good man. He'd walked away from me because, while threatened, he'd done what was best for me. Same went with Claire. He hadn't cared what people thought of him, only of doing the right thing.

And everyone thought he'd been a fuckup. *He'd* thought that of himself.

God, was he so wrong.

"He might not have even left if you hadn't interfered." I was done remaining calm. I was shouting now, wiping at my eyes. I could barely see him through the tears.

"Then you'd have learned what kind of man he was the hard way."

"Like I am now with you."

I was done here. Done with him. Dad had interfered in my relationship with Huck. Broke us up. Destroyed my heart. Let me believe lies.

"Sarah!" he shouted. "You leave and you're done here. You're out. You won't make it in this town as a mechanic. I'll see to it."

I looked back at him. This was what he'd done with

Huck six years ago. But the threat he'd made to Huck had been directed at me. Huck had walked because of the consequences. But now, me?

How had I never seen this side of my dad? I took in his threat. He wanted me to be scared, to tuck my shoulders under and cower. Remember my place. Cede to him. Again.

Now I saw the man for what he was. A loser. He was barely doing his job, slacking because he knew his own daughter would take care of any issues for him. But when things didn't go *just* his way, he got pissed. Tossed out ridiculous threats.

He didn't give a shit about me. Or if he did, he had a horrible way of showing it.

He was the one who was scared. The one who was losing everything, because if I walked, he'd actually have to do some work.

His words had no weight.

I had no idea what I was going to do, but I wasn't afraid any longer. I wasn't going to hold myself back from what I wanted. I knew what it was. *Who* it was.

I didn't say a word, only turned around to leave. I froze in my tracks when I saw Huck. He stood just outside the open garage door, hands on hips. He was in his police uniform, just as I'd seen him on the call before dawn. His eyes were narrowed, his jaw clenched. He wasn't looking at me, but past me to my dad.

My heart lurched and... God. He was here. For me. He seemed bigger. Broader. More intense. Just... more.

He'd walked away all those years ago to make me happy. Now he was here when I needed him most.

I had no idea how much he'd heard, but based on the look on his face, enough.

We both knew the truth of what had happened. How my dad had ripped us apart. How he was willing to do anything to... keep tabs on me? Control me? Steer my life in the direction he wanted it to go?

Huck didn't say anything, just held out his hand. It was right then that I had a choice. I could go to Huck. Take back what we'd lost all those years ago. To take him for the man he was now. Go blindly into a *thing* with Huck based on the man I'd known all those years ago. Not the lies. The whispers. Not even my assumptions, but based on the fact that he'd loved me once. Proved it. Walked away to do so.

I went to him. Put my hand in his, and walked out of the shop.

$\mathcal{H}$UCK

I HELPED her into my police SUV, taking care with her as if she were breakable, even though I was in a rush to get the fuck out of here. Reaching across, I buckled her seat belt. She took my hand, looked up at me, her eyes watery and desperate. "Don't leave."

I gritted my teeth for a second, willing back the desire to go and shoot Bill like a rabid dog. "No, baby girl. No more leaving."

When she released me, I went around and climbed into the driver's seat. I gave the dark garage bay a long look. I didn't see Bill anywhere, but that was fine with me. I didn't want to see the fucker's face again.

He'd made Sarah cry. Said cruel shit. What kind of father gave an ultimatum? That he'd ensure she couldn't get a job in a career she loved solely out of spite? Out of... jealousy? He might set shit in motion, but there was no fucking way he was taking Sarah down. I might have cowered once at his threats. No longer.

Tears slid down her cheeks, but she remained quiet looking out the side window as I cut across town. She had on the same clothes from earlier, jeans and a T-shirt, but she'd ditched the sweatshirt.

I got on the radio with Noreen. "I'm 10-7," I said to her, telling her I was off duty.

"That's what I figured, Chief. We've got you covered, and the other guys will tackle any leftover paperwork."

"Copy that. Thanks."

I took a right at the central intersection on Main.

"It slipped out of gear," she murmured.

I glanced at her, confused. "Huh?"

"Your transmission's going."

I chuckled and slowly shook my head. I knew what she was talking about, the lag, but had never considered what it was. "I can change my truck's oil. Replace a fan belt. That's as far as I can go when it comes to car repairs. As for police vehicles, Noreen takes care of handling any fixes."

With O'Banyons. No fucking longer. I'd learn how to

replace a transmission myself before I gave Bill any more business.

Five minutes later we pulled up in front of Sarah's place. I wanted to take her to the ranch and handcuff *her* to my bed, but I'd dropped Kelsey off only a little while ago. Between Alice, Claire, and Kelsey in the main house, there would be no privacy. The first time I was with Sarah after six years, we'd be alone, that was for fucking sure. And her place was in town and a hell of a lot closer.

"You know where I live," she said, finally looking my way.

"I keep track of those I care about."

I didn't offer her more than that. For now.

I parked, helped her out, led her up the steps to the front door. She lived in a small house in the older section of town. The porch had a swing, and the door was painted a glossy red. She'd been renting it from an older couple who'd moved to Arizona. It was small but all hers. "Give me your keys, baby girl."

She blinked at me. "I left my purse at the shop. I've got a hidden spare."

As she went down the steps to pick up what appeared to be a fake rock from her front flower bed, I called Noreen again, asked her to send someone to O'Banyons to collect Sarah's things. I didn't trust Bill, and I didn't think he'd mess with someone in a uniform.

She opened the door, and I followed her in, shut it behind me. Locked it.

I noticed the size of the room. The color of the walls. The furniture. How neat it was. How it smelled like Sarah. All of it, because that was what I did. Observed. But I didn't look away from my baby girl.

"Huck," she said, then stopped as if other words were stuck.

I didn't say anything, just pulled her into my arms. Hugged her tight like I had at the rollover scene earlier, but this time there wasn't anything between us any longer.

She'd cried then, for coming upon a dead body. It was a shock that I'd sadly gotten used to.

But now she cried for a different reason. There were so many possibilities for the tears. Her dad being an asshole. Learning the truth about what he'd done before she went to college. For what he'd just said to her in the shop. I'd heard every fucking word.

I wanted to punch him in the face. I wanted to rip him to shreds telling him what I thought of him. Fuck, I'd been wanting to do both for so fucking long.

But Bill O'Banyon was nothing to me now. I had Sarah in my arms, and I wasn't letting go.

Her hands came around my back, and she clung to me, cried into my shirt. I stroked her hair, her back, whispered to her how perfect she was. How special. How I'd missed her. Needed her.

I did. I needed Sarah, and holding her was as if I was finally coming alive again. I could feel. See. Breathe. I'd walked away and made something of myself. For her. For me. For my parents. I'd done that, but I'd left a piece of me behind with Sarah. My heart. She hadn't known it. Hell, neither had I. Not until now.

I'd been fourteen when my parents were killed in a plane crash. The last thing I'd said to them had been in anger. We'd fought about stupid teenaged shit, and I'd stormed off, rode an ATV out to the farthest corners of the Manning land. When I'd returned, the then chief of police had stood on the main house front porch with Sawyer and Thatcher to tell me the news. My parents were gone.

I shut down then. Hadn't cared or given a shit about anything. Cut school. Went wild. For years. The person who'd finally tamed me had been Sarah. She'd made me want to be a better person. Lead a life that my parents would be proud of.

I sighed, then kissed the top of her head.

I was exhausted. I'd been woken up for the preschool fire, dealt with Kelsey and Sawyer in the jail, then I'd driven halfway back to the ranch before getting the call for the rollover. The lovebirds had returned first thing for Kelsey to give her statement. That had been followed by the Bunky bombshell and Sawyer punching him in the face and Sawyer stalking out. I'd driven Kelsey to the ranch—yup, she fucking hated me—and then got the call about Sarah's argument with her dad.

Sarah had gone to the rollover and probably hadn't slept since either.

"Come on, baby girl. Let's get some shut-eye."

Her fingers loosened on the back of my shirt, and I led her into her bedroom. Her bed wasn't made, and I had to assume she'd climbed out for the call. A sleep shirt was on the floor and a bra slung over the footboard.

I sat on the side of bed and got her between my knees and began to undo the button on her jeans. Her hand stilled mine, and I lifted my gaze to look into her pale eyes. I saw my whole world there. We had so much to work out between us, but we would. Later.

"You can't sleep in these pants," I murmured. I kept my words soft and gentle. I'd jerked off to the idea of getting her bare more times than I could count, but this wasn't the time to do anything. "Let's get you comfortable. Nothing more."

She let go, and I got the button open, the zipper down. She took over and shimmied the denim down her legs. They caught on her sneakers, and she toed them off, then got rid of her jeans and socks.

Once done she stood in a T-shirt that hit her mid-hip and a pair of pale blue panties, I leaned my forehead against her chest. She was so small, tiny compared to me, that the soft swells of her breasts were a cushion. I breathed her in as I set my hands on the backs of her bare thighs.

It was easy to lift her and turn, settling her into the center of the bed. I stood and set my gun on her nightstand—no kids around for it to be an issue—took off my utility belt, and laid it on top of her dresser. Then I stripped down to my boxers and climbed in beside her, pulled the blankets over us before hooking my arm around her waist and settling her close. I wasn't satisfied until my arm was her pillow and she was tucked up against my side. One of her legs was over mine.

I sighed. Hard.

Fuck yes.

The room was bright with the midday sun, but I didn't give a shit. I was too tired to care, and besides, I had my girl in my arms.

"Sleep, baby girl. I've got you."

───────

SARAH

THE SOUND of my shower woke me. I rolled over, my arm reaching out to where Huck had slept. His spot was warm, meaning he hadn't been up for long. Wiping my eyes, I glanced at the bedside clock. We'd slept for hours. Together.

Just slept.

Being in his arms had been... heaven. I'd felt small and precious. Cared for. Protected. Safe. His dark scent clung to my sheets, and I lifted the pillow he'd used and breathed him in.

Huck.

He was here. He'd come to me when I needed him most. How had he known? How had he just... been there?

I realized it didn't matter. He was naked and in my shower. Using my rose-scented soap. The corner of my mouth tipped up at the thought of a guy as big and brawny as Huck smelling like me. That made me think of the other night when we'd been in his bed. When, while he hadn't been stripped bare, he'd been so attentive. I'd left him with a throbbing hard-on and probably a horrible case of blue balls. That had been my plan. To make him realize how much he'd hurt me.

But in reality he hadn't. He wasn't the one who'd hurt me.

It had been my dad.

I sat up and pushed my messy hair out of my face.

I'd gone to Huck's bed wanting revenge. While I'd responded to his touch, consented to it all, it had been given for a purpose. But Huck had been into it. He'd craved me. Gotten hard and eager enough to let me handcuff him to his headboard because he wanted me.

He'd eaten me out because my pleasure had been his sole goal.

Huck Manning still desired me as much as I desired him. It was time to make a decision about what I truly wanted from Huck. I'd had six years thinking the worst of him but only a short time to know the truth. I wasn't who I'd been back then. Neither was Huck. I didn't really know much about this older version of him.

But I knew *him.*

Huck Manning was in my shower. Did I want him as much as I had all those years ago? I wasn't nineteen any longer. Not an innocent young woman who was infatuated with the rugged older cowboy. After what my dad had done, how I'd not gone to Huck and talked to him about Claire, he still wanted me. No guy would wash with rose soap otherwise.

I climbed from the bed and pushed the bathroom door open. Steam billowed over the top of the shower curtain. His boxers were on the yellow bath mat.

I took off my T-shirt, bra, and panties and slid back the shower curtain. I wanted Huck for all the right reasons now. It was time to show him that.

13

 ARAH

*S*UNDAY *NIGHT*

HUCK WAS NAKED. Wet. I took in the strong back muscles. Soap bubbles sliding down over his taut butt. He turned. Then my mouth went dry. I stared. I couldn't help it. I shouldn't objectify the man by ogling his body.

But... holy shit.

I couldn't look away from his broad torso, the rock-hard abs. The jutting cock that was thick and long and now aimed straight at me.

He'd been inside me. Once. We'd made out for months, getting hotter and heavier until that night in the back of his truck. It had changed everything for me. Gave me something that had come from our love, even if only for a short time.

"Joining me, baby girl?" he asked when I hadn't moved, my hand still on the shower curtain.

It pulled my thoughts back to the present. Finally I met Huck's gaze. Saw the question there. The heat. The amusement. I couldn't help but smile, and knew what he was asking wasn't as simple as me stepping into my tub.

Was I joining Huck? For good? Because I knew this was it. Huck was all in. He could've snuck out while I slept. He could've never come to O'Banyons.

I'd made up my mind when I took his hand at the shop, so I stepped in beside him, slid the curtain closed behind us. His body blocked me from the hot spray.

He set one hand on the tile behind me, the other on my hip, lowered his head, and kissed me. His lips were insistent, and his tongue immediately plunged and found mine.

He growled, low and deep, as he drove me wild with just his mouth. He angled his head, took more. His whiskers rasped my skin as he kissed along my jaw to my ear.

"Baby girl, what you do to me," he murmured, then nipped the spot where my neck and shoulder met.

Stepping closer, he set his knee between mine, his dick pressing long and thick against my belly.

"Huck," I whispered, my eyes closed, my head angled back to give him room. I was more aroused from just a kiss from Huck than having sex with another guy. Neither previous lover had gotten me off. Only Huck had been able to do it, and I was close now. My breasts ached. My nipples were hard. My pussy longed for his touch. To be filled. It was as if my body remembered him.

His lips returned to mine, devoured me. His hand slid up my body to cup my jaw. I felt the callouses, how big his palm was. He pulled back, and I blinked my eyes open. He was right there, his pale eyes so close I saw the darker flecks. The heat. His gaze dipped and roved over my body.

We were breathing hard as we just... looked.

We'd gotten naked that night in his truck bed, but it had been dark. The only light had been from the sliver of the moon, and I'd seen him, but not like this. He was so much more than I remembered.

I hadn't even realized I'd pressed my hands to the shower wall behind me until I couldn't resist touching him. As I set my palms on his chest, he sucked in a breath, his abs going tight. I slid my fingers down over the ridges, then lower still to grip his thick length. His dick was hot and like steel.

"Fuck," he growled.

My gaze whipped up, and I caught the look on his face. The clenched jaw, the narrowed eyes. The heat in them.

I wasn't the virgin any longer. While I'd been with two guys since Huck, I didn't even remember their faces. They'd been placeholders as I waited for Huck and me to be together again. Nothing more.

Now I thought of pleasing Huck. He'd made me feel good the other night. It was time for me to have a turn. He was slick in my hold, and I worked my grip up and down his length, running my thumb over the broad crown each time. Gently I cupped his balls with my other hand.

Huck's head dropped and he held himself still, but when I started to lower to my knees so I could take him into my mouth, he gripped my elbow.

I looked to him, frowned.

"You might have your hand on my dick, but I'm still in charge, baby girl. You'll get me off with your hand because I'm a few pumps away from spurting over your belly. I'm okay with that because I gotta get that first one out of the way so I can take my time with you."

I went to work, gripped him in both my hands. He was so big my fingers barely closed and long enough where I could still get strokes in. God, it was so hot watching him lose his firm control.

He swore under his breath. Growled. His hips bucked, and he slapped his hand against the wet tile as he came. His body shuddered as thick ropes of his cum pulsed onto my belly. I only stopped when his hand gripped my wrist.

His breath was ragged, and it took him a few long seconds to recover. Looking into my eyes, he shifted so the hot spray washed my stomach clean. Then he reached back, shut off the water, and yanked the shower curtain open. With hands on my waist, he lifted me and set me on the bath mat. Following me out, he grabbed a towel and dried me off, then gave himself a quick rubdown.

"Bed. Now." I turned in that direction, eager. I was wet and not from the shower. His hand came down on my butt, a light smack that had me gasping.

I looked over my shoulder and he grinned. "Yeah, that's what I thought."

It seemed something in my eyes gave me away. Besides being startled by the single spank, I was also turned on by it. Who knew?

Huck.

"I want you in that bed, knees bent, legs spread nice and wide so I can see all of you."

I flicked my gaze down to his cock, which was hard and ready as if he hadn't just come.

"I took you once, nice and gentle. You ready to see how it's really like between us? I took you missionary so I could take your cherry and watch your face as I did it. Now that's not going to be enough. For either of us."

I bit my lip, took in the huge naked guy filling my tiny bathroom. "I want more," I confirmed.

A flush spread down his cheeks, and his eyes went dark and intense. He pointed. "Bed. Now."

My father had told me what to do and what to be, and I'd hated it. But a few dirty words that were bossy as hell from Huck and I felt safe. Empowered. Beautiful.

There was a world of difference when I gave myself to the right person. I had a feeling I was about to find out just how much.

———

HUCK

HOLY FUCK. I had never come so hard before, and that had just been a hand job. I swore I'd gone blind there for a second. I took a moment in the bathroom to come to grips with where I was. Who I was with. What we were about to do.

I'd made Sarah mine six years ago. It was time to do so again.

This time, nothing was going to tear us apart.

I left the bathroom, and there she was, just as I'd ordered. Sarah was bare and beautiful, legs bent, knees spread.

I took in every inch of her. From the wild blonde curls on her head to the little patch at the top of her pink pussy.

Fuck me.

Stalking over, I climbed up onto the bed, crawled on top of her, loomed. Looked down at her. Took in the trusting eyes, the flushed cheeks. I shifted lower and surveyed her perfect tits. I couldn't resist sucking a little nipple into my mouth and giving it a tug.

Her hands dived into my hair. Clung. Tugged.

"Huck!" she cried.

I lifted my head. "What is it, baby girl? What do you want?"

"You."

"You've got me."

"In me," she added.

"Gotta get you ready first."

She squirmed. "I'm ready."

I shook my head. "If you remember, I'm big and your pussy's a tight little thing."

"I'm not a virgin anymore," she reminded.

I hadn't asked if she'd been with anyone else besides me. While I assumed it was a yes, I wasn't going to ask. I hadn't been celibate either. The time that had come between when I made her mine and now was in the past. She was mine. She was beneath me. That was all that mattered.

"You want me to take you hard?" Just asking her the

question made my dick pulse. I had all kinds of ideas on how I wanted to fuck Sarah.

She nodded.

"I'm going to eat you out, get you nice and soft and wet and ready for my dick. Then I'll fuck you. On your back. On all fours. Over the edge of the bed. Hell, against the wall. All night long."

"Please."

I leaned down, kissed her nipple, then the other. "That's right, I love to hear you beg. But it's a little early yet."

Shifting down her body, I gripped one thigh, then the other, spread her wide, and settled my shoulders between. Breathing her in, I looked my fill. *My pussy.*

She was wet and eager for me.

"Shit," I muttered, shaking my head. "I don't have a condom."

Fuck me. My girl was naked and spread and ready, and I didn't have anything to protect her.

"I do."

I arched a brow, narrowed my gaze.

"They came in a party favor bag from a bachelorette party. It's in my bedside drawer."

Reaching over, I yanked it open and found her stash. There were at least five. That would hold us... for a few hours. I ripped one open, slid it on.

"Huck," she whimpered when I finished.

I'd gotten off in the shower. She hadn't.

I didn't make her wait any longer. While I might tease her someday, she was being a good girl and deserved all the orgasms I could give her.

I licked down her seam, then used my thumbs to part her, then licked her again, from her dripping opening to her clit. I'd figured out what got her hot on Friday night, but now I had my hands and slipped two fingers into her. Found her G-spot when she arched her back and cried out my name.

I worked her hard. Watched what made her gasp, writhe, clutch at my hair, and did it again. And again. She came quickly, her pussy gushing onto my palm.

Before she finished coming, I worked my way up her body, positioned myself at her entrance, and slid home.

"Fuck!" I groaned, her pussy walls clenching down, practically strangling my dick as she continued to come. I pulled back, thrust deep again. When her legs wrapped around my hips, her heels digging into my ass, I took her hard. Our skin slapped together. Her tits swayed. Her eyes met mine. Held as she lifted her hips to meet me.

I pulled all the way out, then flipped Sarah onto her stomach. With my hand hooked around her waist, I pulled her back onto her knees, pressed into her from behind.

"Huck!" she cried. This angle made it easy to go

extra deep. She had all of me now. I felt every inch of her clamping down.

"Good girl. Take me." I slapped her ass, and a pink handprint instantly bloomed. She clenched. "Fuck."

I spanked her again, and she reached down beneath her and began to play with her clit.

Holy shit. My girl owned her passion. She knew what she wanted, what she needed. Another time I'd punish her for touching *my* pussy, but not now.

She was wild. Uninhibited. If she needed to play with her clit to get off... this time, I was going to fuck her hard and watch it happen.

Which I did, until I came right along with her and we lost all thought together. It wasn't the only time we fucked. I'd meant every word about how I would take her. I didn't want her to ever doubt I did what I said. If that meant using up all those condoms, then so be it.

14

*S*ARAH

AFTER THE LAST round of sex, Huck passed out. I'd fallen asleep in his arms, but only for a short time. My hunger woke me, and it wasn't for Huck. This time. I slipped on my sleep shirt I'd found on the floor and pulled together something to eat. It was after ten. It was dark out the kitchen window, only adding to the feel of being in a little bubble. Just me and Huck. There was so much outside of this house we had to face, had to talk about. It was coming, and soon.

For now I chopped the peppers and onions I'd pulled from the fridge for an omelet. I was sore in interesting places. My pussy ached, completely unused to being taken so thoroughly. Red marks barely ringed my wrists because he'd pulled his handcuffs out and put them to use on me this time. Fortunately his revenge was to get me close to coming over and over, then pulling back. He was inventive and ruthless and... sexy as hell. And his dick?

"I like seeing you happy."

I turned my head at Huck standing in the doorway, and I couldn't help but smile even more. He was in his jeans and nothing else, the top button undone. I didn't glimpse the waistband of his boxers, which meant he was right there... easy access.

"I see that hungry look in your eye. And it's not for whatever you're making."

I gave a slight shrug. "I can't help it if you're so jumpable."

He grinned. "Jumpable?"

After he took a few steps in my direction with an intention in his gaze that indicated he was hungry for something and it wasn't eggs, I pointed the small knife at him and narrowed my eyes.

"Stay back until I've eaten."

He raised his hands, but the grin didn't slip as he settled onto one of my kitchen chairs.

"It's good to know we worked up your appetite."

I didn't respond because it was true—oh so true— and got back to work, finished the chopping, grabbed the eggs, and cracked them into a bowl.

"This place suits you," he said. I looked his way as he took in my small kitchen.

"Thanks. After school and being on my own for years, there was no way I was moving back in with my dad. I realize now I hadn't drawn much of a line where he was concerned in my life, except for where I lived."

"About your dad," he said, his voice quiet. He didn't say more as I poured the eggs into the hot pan on the stove. The butter made them sizzle and pop.

"Yeah. My dad."

I picked up a spatula and lifted the corner of the cooking eggs. I focused on the omelet as he sat quietly, just content to watch.

It didn't take long before the late-night meal was ready. I sliced it and split it between two plates. I carried both to the table and sat beside him. Other than my dad, I'd never had a guy in my house before, and he'd never stayed for a meal.

But now I had Huck, who dwarfed my table, scarfing down my impromptu dinner without a shirt on.

"I'm sorry about what he said to you," Huck said eventually, after wiping his mouth with a napkin he'd pulled from the holder in the center of the table.

"Which part?"

"The ultimatum."

I stabbed a piece of pepper, ate it. My dad had

made me choose. Him or Huck. Him or no chance of running my own shop in The Bend.

"Yeah, well, it's not the first one he's given where I'm concerned."

My eyes met Huck's. I waited for him to confirm what my dad had said.

"No, it wasn't."

I dropped my fork onto my plate, took a sip of water although my hand shook, and Huck didn't miss it. He grabbed the glass, set it down.

"Walking away from you was one of the hardest things I've ever done." He ran a hand over his head, his eyes bleak.

I wasn't hungry any longer, and I pushed the plate back.

This was the wound that had cut us both deep and obviously hadn't healed. There'd been only a scab over it for six years, and my dad had decided to rip that sucker right off.

Now we were both hurting all over again, bleeding with emotions that we'd kept inside.

It was a gross thought, but it was strangely what I imagined.

"I'd have gone," I said. "Left with you."

He shook his head, reached out and took my hand, set them on the table between us. "I know. And I'd have paid for your school."

"Then—"

"He's your daddy," he replied, cutting me off. "Your family. You have your sister."

I gave a little laugh. Lynn was five years older, and because of that age gap, we'd never been all that close. She went off to college when I was in seventh grade, and married Bunky the summer after graduation. It had only been me and my dad for a long time.

"I know what it's like to lose a parent," he continued. "To not have them in your life."

Both of his had died years before we met. I'd been a little kid then. I knew the loss ate at him, that he'd been so lost in his grief. The Mannings were a close family. Tight. Maybe because the tragedy had pulled them together, but from what I'd heard of his parents, they'd been good people and *made* good boys.

Somehow he'd seen something in me that soothed him, eased that hurt. I couldn't replace them, but I'd given him a... connection he'd lost.

"Why didn't you tell me the truth?"

"Even if you believed me, it would have torn you two apart."

"But I could have made that decision myself." I got mad, remembering how devastated I'd been. I popped up from my chair, grabbed my plate, and carried it to the sink. Turning, I leaned against the counter.

His gaze raked down my legs, which were bare. My sleep T-shirt only came to midthigh.

"Don't you think I should have known about what

my dad was like? He threatened you. Us. Just like today."

"He was scared. Afraid of losing you."

My eyes widened. "You're defending him?"

Sighing, he crooked a finger for me to come to him. For a second I refused, but I went nonetheless. I stepped between his parted knees. With one hand at my waist, he pulled me down onto his lap so I strad-dled him.

"No fucking way. But having Claire has given me some perspective. If there's a guy sniffing around her when she's eighteen who I think isn't good enough for her, I might do something similar."

"No, you wouldn't," I countered. His hands moved to my hips, settled there. His strong thighs were my seat, and this close I could see the dark flecks in his blue eyes. He still hadn't shaved, and the whiskers coming in were darker than that on his head. And chest.

One dark eyebrow winged up. "Oh yeah?"

"Because you're going to raise a strong woman who can decide if a guy's worthy of her all on her own. And if not, she'll throat punch him."

He frowned, clearly not thrilled with that idea, although the way his mouth turned up at the corner, he'd probably be showing her the throat punch move soon.

"I found a worthy guy all on my own," I said,

setting a hand over Huck's chest. I felt the steady beat of his heart. I looked up at him through my lashes. "My dad didn't think it. *You* didn't think it either."

He didn't say anything for a long time. "Baby girl... I was lost back then. You helped me find my way out. But it wasn't enough. You needed to go to school. Follow your dream. I'd hoped... thought that after I finished the academy, you'd come to me. I know it's stupid, but I did."

"But you brought Claire home."

He nodded.

"Tell me what happened."

"Mandy, her mother, was a neighbor. I... I didn't take our breakup that well. When I wasn't at the academy, I was lost in a bottle of whiskey. I drank too much. Blacked out. One of those times, I woke up and found her in my apartment. She said we'd fucked."

I stiffened in his lap but didn't say anything.

"I remembered nothing. For good reason too because it actually never happened." His jaw clenched as if talking about it pissed him off. "Three weeks later she came to me saying she was pregnant. I had no intention of marrying her, but she—I thought—was making my kid. I wanted that baby."

My skin prickled with heat, my cheeks flushing. Pain lanced through me remembering the baby we'd actually made. The one I'd wanted.

"I went to the hospital after the birth and overheard her saying I wasn't the real father. That she didn't know who it was, but the Manning name on the birth certificate would ensure she was set for life." His fingers tightened around my waist.

"Oh my God," I whispered, imagining Huck, eager for his new baby and finding out it had all been a lie.

"She'd been irresponsible while pregnant, and I got pictures. Proof of it. Then when I learned the truth, I couldn't let her raise a child. I decided Claire was mine. I learned a thing or two at the academy. Made some friends. I had Kale petition the court for sole custody because of what I'd pulled together. I'll skip all the legal crap, but a judge's ruling and a pile of cash had Mandy walking. She'd never wanted a kid."

"So you graduated and came home with Claire. She's legally yours." He nodded. "The birth certificate says you're the father."

"Yeah."

"You didn't care what people said about you?"

"My family knew. But off the ranch, I only cared what you thought. And you never came."

Tears welled in my eyes and spilled. He sighed, lifted his hands, and wiped them away with his thumbs. He didn't know the true reason for the tears. He'd gotten a baby while the one I'd carried, the one he'd really made, had died. I hadn't known the truth of his situation, but the loss I felt never went away.

"So much lost time."

He pulled me down so I leaned into him, my head on his shoulder. I stared at my fridge but thought of what could have been.

"I can't wish things went differently because then I wouldn't have Claire. I only wish you hadn't gotten hurt."

He was always watching out for me. Protecting me. That was why I loved it when he called me *baby girl*. I didn't have a daddy fetish, but I knew that whenever I was with Huck, that I was safe. He'd take care of me.

"Everything that happened, happened *not* because of us. The one thing that was real was us. Then—"

His eyes flared in understanding. "And now."

"I have no idea what I'm going to do."

He frowned. "With your daddy? He didn't mean it."

"I think he did."

"It doesn't make it right."

"No."

"You've got a strong little business going."

My lip turned up. "How do you know that?"

His hand slid around the back of my neck, cupped me there. "I've kept track of you."

All this time he'd been watching me from afar.

"You want to run a shop. You always have. You should do it," he suggested.

And he remembered my dreams.

This man. God, Huck Manning was my beginning and my end.

His fingers tangled in my hair and gave a gentle tug. It lit up every nerve ending in my body. "Baby girl, you take what you want in life."

I had a feeling he might want me. No, I knew he did. But forever?

I pulled my lips to the side, bit my bottom lip. "I know. *I know.* I thought I'd do it with my dad. But if I start my own shop, he'll be *really* mad. Definitely try to blacklist me."

"A father shouldn't keep his child from fulfilling her dreams. Or tearing them down." His hand loosened in my hair, and he slid it down my back, cupped my butt. "He can try all he wants. I know who the police department will be calling for tow services. And you fixed that tractor when no one else could. Your daddy doesn't touch farm equipment."

I grinned then, remembering that old tractor and how no one could get it to run but me.

"I'd say you'd have a business in house calls alone," he added.

It was an interesting idea. A mobile repair shop.

"Come to the ranch with me. Meet Claire."

He'd switched topics, probably because I wasn't going to decide to start a new business sitting on his lap in my kitchen.

But meet his child? The one that was supposed to be ours? I wasn't ready to share that secret. I couldn't. I hadn't told anyone. But if I wanted to be with Huck, it included Claire.

I nodded. "Okay."

He leaned in, brushed his nose with mine. He smelled of my rose soap and himself. "First, I'm going to fuck you again. Make sure you know you're mine." He spread his knees wider, which parted my legs even more. He reached between my thighs and cupped me. "That you know this pussy's mine."

I let my eyes fall closed as his touch became more deliberate. Urgent. When he slipped a finger into me and found me wet, who was I to complain?

$\mathcal{H}$UCK

I PULLED up in front of the main house and parked. Sitting there, I counted to ten in my head. Sarah glanced at me from the passenger seat, wondering why I hadn't gotten out of the car. I only made it to seven before the screen door flew open and Claire ran out, jumping the last two steps off the front porch. She had on her usual jeans and sneakers and a blue T-shirt.

A grin was impossible to avoid as I took in her exuberance to see me. This was our routine, as I usually texted Alice to let her know I was leaving the station. I knew her eagerness to see me wasn't going to last forever, so I was enjoying it while I could.

"Ready?" I asked, taking Sarah's hand and giving it a squeeze.

She didn't look my way, but at the approaching five-year-old.

I climbed from the police SUV and rounded the back, ready for my little girl's hug, which was often more like a body tackle. But she wasn't there. She'd gone to Sarah's side and wiggled about as Sarah shut the door behind her.

"You bought my daddy?" Claire asked, looking up at Sarah with such eagerness and glee. On Saturday, when Kelsey had come to visit Sawyer, Claire had been ecstatic thinking her preschool teacher was going to be her new mother. Kelsey'd been sweet and deflected, but it made me realize how eager Claire was for a mother.

Sarah leaned down and gave Claire a kind smile. Her eyes were watery with tears, and she was blinking hard to will them back. This moment would be a mental picture for me. The woman I loved—yeah, Sarah had my fucking heart—and my little girl. Together. Finally.

"I did buy him."

Claire clapped her small hands, then gave Sarah the body-tackle hug I'd expected. Sarah looked to me as she wrapped her arms around Claire. "Yay, then you're my new mommy!"

"Claire," I warned. My heart skipped a beat at the

possibility.

The night before, after we'd talked over the omelette, I'd checked in with Alice and let her know I was staying the night with Sarah. I didn't usually share that I was spending the night with a woman to the Manning housekeeper/mother hen/grandmother. Hell, I'd never spent the night with a woman before. Sex, yes, but I'd never lingered.

And I sure as hell had never brought one home. Until now.

Alice must have told Claire I would be bringing someone to the ranch with me this morning.

"Claire Manning, please use your big girl manners," I said. While I gave my words a slight bite of warning, the smile on my lips indicated I was pleased with her eagerness.

I was. I had no idea how crucial it was for Claire to like—no, love—Sarah as much as me.

Claire stepped back and tipped her chin up to look Sarah in the eye. Even though Sarah was five-foot-nothing, she had some height over my daughter.

"Hello. I'm Claire Manning. It's nice to meet you."

Pride swelled my chest at her good manners, even if they were a little late.

The slap of the screen door had me looking to the porch and Alice. She knew Sarah. Hell, she knew everyone in town. She put a hand on the porch rail and looked very happy by our arrival. Or at least Sarah's.

"I'm pleased to meet you, too. I'm Sarah."

"Are you my new mommy?" Claire asked again.

"Claire, is that a proper thing to ask someone you just met?" I asked, going over to her and ruffling her blonde hair, which this morning was pulled back into two pigtails.

"You said you were working on it, and now she's here," Claire said, scrunching up her face.

I blushed because those were the words I'd used on Saturday morning. I actually fucking blushed at that, but a quick glance at Sarah and I knew she was enchanted.

"I'm your new friend. How about that?" Sarah offered instead.

Claire smiled and nodded. Then her eyes widened as if she'd remembered something important. "I have puppies! I show all my friends the puppies!"

"Claire, a hostess offers her friends a drink when they come to visit," Alice reminded from the porch.

"Would you like a drink to carry while we go see the puppies in the stable?" Claire wiggled and bounced with her usual excitement and took Sarah's hand and began to tug.

I shook my head, amused. "I'm going to go get changed," I told Sarah, tipping my head toward the house. I had on the same clothes from the fire and rollover calls on Saturday night. "I'll catch up with you both in a few. And I'll bring drinks."

"All right," Sarah said. She looked to Alice, offered her a wave as she finally let Claire lead her. Hand in hand.

I watched them for a minute, two blonde-haired beauties, heading down the drive to the stable, then went up onto the porch.

"I'm glad she's here, Huck," Alice said, setting her hand on my shoulder.

Looking down at the older woman, I placed my hand on top of hers. Felt the strength in it. She'd done so much for me and my brothers. For the ranch. Her plan was to retire to Alabama to be near her sister, but she wanted us happily wed—or at least paired off—before she did.

"So?" she asked, a hint of hope lacing the word.

"I'm working on it."

———————

SARAH

I SAT in the straw and watched Claire with the new puppies. They were probably eight or nine weeks old, fat and roly-poly but sound asleep. They were sprawled and clumped around their mother. I petted the dog's soft head as she slept, too. If I had all those babies to watch and feed, I'd be exhausted as well.

One little human like Claire was a bunch of energy and excitement. She hadn't stopped talking since she barreled out of her house. Her hair was the same fair color as Huck's, which had deceived me all this time. They looked blood related.

But this happy five-year-old was where she belonged. She had her daddy but also Alice, Sawyer, and Thatcher. The others who lived and worked on the ranch. A family.

"Don't you think?" Claire asked, carefully picking up a sleeping puppy and setting it in her lap. The animal stirred but didn't wake up. She was looking at me with eager blue eyes. Her face was round, her nose a pert button, and those cheeks were flushed with excitement. One of her pigtails drooped a little.

I smiled at her. "What, sweetheart?"

"Daddy said I can keep one even though they're Uncle Thatch's babies since Maple's his dog. I think this one's Sandy, don't you?" She stared down at the puppy with such love, but her look shifted to the rest of the brood.

"Sandy?" I asked.

Claire rolled her eyes at me with the skill of a four-teen-year-old. Since it was followed up with a giggle, it was teenage drama-free.

"The one I'm keeping. I've named her Sandy."

They were various shades of tan except for one black puppy, which could probably be ruled out. Claire said Sandy was a girl, but I wasn't going to weed out the girls from the boys from the sleeping bunch to narrow it down. A little lesson in the birds and the bees wasn't for me to tackle. Her mother would—

Oh.

She didn't have a mother. She had Alice, who I knew would guide Claire on girl stuff. She didn't need too much advice at this age, but out here on the ranch, I was sure she'd learned she couldn't pee standing up like her daddy and uncles.

But Alice was more of a grandmother to the girl, and Claire seemed eager, almost desperate, for a mother. I could relate since while mine had been around when I was Claire's age, she hadn't stuck. She'd left about two years after. I'd been raised by my dad. And look where that had gotten me.

"Is she?" Claire asked, impatient.

I nodded. "She's the cutest one, for sure."

She looked down at Sandy and gently petted her. The joy on her face was so open and easy.

"Your daddy's pretty nice, isn't he?" I asked.

She nodded and scrunched up her nose. "He watches out for everyone in the *whole* town."

"He does."

"If you're going to be my mommy, then you have to be in love with my daddy."

My heart leaped, but I remained calm. She wasn't prying. When she looked up at me with eyes that were filled with sly curiosity, I had to rethink it. She *was* prying, but she was just a little girl.

"Why do you say that?" I asked, petting Maple.

"Daddy told me he wanted a love like my Nana and PopPop had. I never met them. They're in heaven."

Oh shit. Tears filled my eyes, but I willed them back as she chattered on.

"They made a love so good that my daddy wants one just like that. I heard him say to Seesaw that he had it once, but it was gone."

I didn't know who Seesaw was, but that wasn't what I focused on. *He had it once.*

"But maybe Nana bought PopPop like Seesaw bought Kelsey and you bought Daddy." She looked up at me, and her eyes flared wide with excitement. "That's it! He was just waiting for you to pay for him."

I didn't know what to say to that. The girl was young but perceptive. Had Huck been waiting for me to buy him? Had that been what we'd needed to get back together?

"If you're my mommy, then you can make me a brother. Alice said a baby comes from a mommy's nangina and you have one." She nodded her little head and snuggled Sandy closer.

I sputtered at her lack of filter, then sucked in a breath. She wanted me and Huck to make a sibling for her.

I hopped to my feet and sniffed. We'd used

condoms the night before, and I'd been so hot for Huck I hadn't thought about the consequences of what would happen if one failed... again. It was impossible to keep the tears back now, and I didn't want Claire to see me like this. "I'll be just outside for a minute."

I fled the horse stall and bumped into someone. Hands grabbed my arms. "Easy there." I blinked the tears away to find Thatcher. "I came to check on Maple and the—" His easy smile slipped away. "You okay, darlin'?"

I nodded absently. "Will you... will you stay with Claire?" I asked, not wanting to leave the little girl unsupervised.

He studied my face as if he could read my problems. "Sure thing."

I walked off, out the far side of the stable, and leaned against the wall. I let the tears fall then. Cute, sassy, whip-smart Claire could have been mine. Mine and Huck's. The blonde curls. The blue eyes. The sassy disposition. She wouldn't have ever considered her daddy being bought. If she were the baby we'd made— even accidentally—she'd know she'd been created from love. A connection like her Nana's and PopPop's.

I started walking, cutting through the tall grass, blind to which direction I was going. Huck believed all the secrets between us had been shared. That my dad's threat and Huck's acquiescence was the only thing that had kept us apart. But there was one secret that I still held. It was a loss that couldn't be fixed or worked through. He deserved to know the truth. Now, especially. I just wasn't sure how I was going to break it to Huck that he'd lost more that day he'd walked away than he ever realized.

 UCK

I'D BARELY GOTTEN out of the shower when I got a text from Noreen letting me know Lynn Bunker called in to make a police report that her car had been stolen from the grocery store parking lot.

Water dripped down my back as I sent her a 10-4 back, informing her I saw the message. She hadn't texted for me to be on the lookout for the fancy car. I was sure it was on to some chop shop somewhere by now. She'd texted because she knew I was with Sarah and probably wanted to tell her. We hadn't talked about how close she was with Lynn these days, but we'd get there. I also thought that Bunky'd had some pretty shitty luck this weekend.

I was halfway to the barn in fresh jeans, T-shirt, and boots when I got another text, this one from Thatcher. Sarah was crying and had ducked out the back side of the stable. I couldn't imagine how a five-year-old and a bunch of puppies would upset her, but she and I had dealt with some heavy shit the past few days.

I'd gotten two texts in about fifteen minutes. It wasn't impossible that her dad had reached out and fucked with her some more.

I picked up my pace and detoured around the building instead of going inside, knowing my brother would take care of Claire. I stopped when I saw Sarah in the distance, sitting on a boulder in the middle of the field.

The sun made her hair look like threads of gold, and the way it caught the breeze... she was perfect here. She'd been on the ranch before, so long ago now. I'd wanted her here. Saw her being on the ranch permanently.

I headed in her direction again and dropped down beside her on the warmed rock. Our sides touched. She wasn't crying, but the evidence of it was there. Flushed cheeks, red eyes. A bleakness about her that said she carried something heavy. I wanted to take it from her. All her problems. I was fucking strong enough to do it.

"Baby girl, what's the matter?"

She tilted her head, rested it against my shoulder. "Claire's perfect."

I couldn't help but smile. "I think so."

"You better put a collar on one of those puppies soon, otherwise she's going to want to keep them all. Even the black one."

"You mean Sandy, Sandra, Sandrine, Sandor, and—"

"Sandor?" She looked up, a pale brow arched.

"Colonel Sanders?" I added, hoping to make her smile.

"She's so smart, Huck. I bet she's going to figure out how to tuck that dog into her backpack and take her to kindergarten."

I tipped her chin up with my finger. "I took a frog. Thatcher somehow took the feral barn cat."

"It runs in the family then." Her smile slipped, and her gaze shifted away.

"Look at me," I murmured. It took a few seconds, but she glanced back. "What's the matter?"

"I... I have something to tell you." She pulled at my hold, and I dropped my hand.

I braced myself, unsure of what she was going to say. Whatever it was—and it seemed bad if it made her cry—we'd deal with it together. I waited, recognizing I needed to be patient.

"You were it for me."

My stomach dropped. "Baby girl, I *am* it for you."

"When you left, I was destroyed. At first I thought you were just chicken."

I frowned and it actually made her smile.

"I *thought* you were pushing me away because you couldn't handle it. In the back of your pickup, we'd just—"

"I took your cherry. As I did so, I said you were mine."

"I know," she whispered.

"You didn't believe me?" I reached up, stroked her hair back.

"In the moment I did. It was perfect, Huck. But after, I thought... I don't know what I thought. The next summer when I came home, you had Claire."

"We talked this through already," I said. It had been hard enough in her kitchen. Doing it again now was like messing with a wound and keeping it from healing.

"Remember I said I thought you left me and slept with someone else right after?"

"It wasn't true," I reminded.

"I thought you got someone pregnant."

"I didn't."

"You had a baby." She glanced away. "Without me."

I stilled.

"Sarah," I murmured, kissing the top of her head. "You want to make a baby? We'll have as many as you want."

Tears filled her eyes. "I made a baby." Her blue gaze lifted to mine. "With you."

I stared at her. Confused. "What?"

"That night, I got pregnant."

I hopped up as if the rock was made of lava. Walked away, then spun around and came back. "You... we... what?"

She cried now, but I couldn't go to her. Not yet. I didn't understand.

"I found out I was pregnant after I moved into the dorm. But I miscarried a few weeks later."

The feeling... fuck. There was a piece of me I didn't even know I had inside that revealed itself now. It hurt. Throbbed. Ached.

I went to her, dropped down onto the grass in front of her feet. "Baby girl. Oh God." I ran a hand over my face. She'd been pregnant. Alone. Lost the baby. And me. "I'm sorry. I'm so, so sorry."

I pulled her into my arms so she was in my lap. I held her tight as she cried, as I mourned the loss of a baby I'd never even known we'd made. Then it all became clear.

"Claire would be the same age."

She nodded against my chest, wiped her nose on my shirt.

"You saw Claire and not only thought I'd been with someone else, but that she could have been ours."

I held her then, giving her the comfort she'd needed from me all those years ago. The summer breeze blew past us, the sound of it rustling the tall grass. What she'd endured and lost was so much greater than I'd imagined. I ached for the child we'd made and would never know. I remembered seeing Claire for the first time. Her bald little head, the tiny fingers. I'd thought I'd made her then. Only an hour later I'd learned the truth. I hadn't cared. I couldn't change that she'd become mine the instant I laid eyes on her.

But Sarah had carried the baby inside her. Loved it before she even knew what it was. Because we'd made it that night. Together.

"I wore a condom, but obviously that had failed. But I'm glad."

"That the baby died?" she asked, tipping her head up to give me her confused eyes.

"That we made something that was a part of both of us. Our baby was loved, baby girl."

Tears lodged in my throat. I'd had a child, and I hadn't even known it. The loss was sinking in. I kissed her, wanting to be as close to her as possible. To let her feel me, know I was holding her. That we were meant to be, that I craved her. Not just her body but her heart. The child she'd carried for us. I, too, was grieving the loss of what could have been. The child we'd lost.

"I loved you," I told her, dotting my lips across her brow. "Then. I love you now. Nothing can replace the baby we lost. Not Claire, not any baby we make. But I promise I'll be with you from now on. *Nothing* will keep us apart."

"I... I love you, too. I want to try again," she admitted.

I'd thought Claire would be my only child. Being blessed with her was good enough for me, but getting Sarah back, making a family with her?

"You want to make a baby with me?"

She nodded. "I'm not sure about five though."

I laughed then, wiped my eyes because they were filled with tears like hers. "We can ditch the condoms and work on it all you want. But I want a ring on your finger if we're going to put a baby in your belly."

She smiled then, brilliantly. Even with her cheeks splotchy and the weight of our loss heavy on my soul, this was one of the most perfect moments.

Sarah was mine, and she'd have my name. And give me our child.

17

*S*ARAH

I SAT in Huck's arms for a while. Keeping me on his lap, he'd settled back against the rock. We talked. Whispered. Kissed. There was no ring, but we were engaged. There was no sex, so we hadn't made a baby, but we would. We had our entire lives before us. Together.

Eventually we got up and made our way back to the stable hand in hand. Huck didn't seem to want to let me go, and I was content with that. We peeked in on Maple and the puppies, but they were alone and nursing. We walked up to the main house, but it was quiet.

Huck assumed Alice had gone into town with Thatcher and Claire.

Whenever I thought of the baby, I'd think of it as the one *we'd* lost. I wasn't alone now. I would carry my own grief about it and so would Huck. But we had each other to lean on now.

And it wasn't a secret any longer. The baby wasn't mine to hide.

"Stay with me," he said, tugging me so I was pulled into his arms again. His lips settled on the top of my head as he hugged me. "Stay here on the ranch."

"What about Claire? And Alice?"

"I'm thirty-two years old. I'm not sixteen trying to sneak you in. Besides, Alice is the one who put me in the bachelor auction in the first place. It's all her fault."

I couldn't help but laugh as I tipped my head back and looked up at him. "Her fault?"

"She'll take the credit, I'm sure."

"And Claire?"

"She's little. She just wants you to be her mommy. You good with that?"

Have a five-year-old? I smiled. "I'm good with that. Then yes, I want to stay here with you."

"Let's go get a few of your things. We can figure out the rest."

He held the door open for me as I climbed into the passenger seat of his police SUV, then leaned in and buckled my seat belt. Then kissed me.

I could do my own belt. Huck knew it, but I loved the gesture, saying without words that he'd always protect me. I certainly didn't mind the kiss or the look in his eyes that promised more.

As we headed into town, I thought of Huck. Us. Claire. Everything. But I was happy. I'd always wanted this, to be with him. To have a family. We'd just taken a really big detour. Not all our problems were solved. My dad was going to be difficult.

"I forgot to tell you, your sister put in a police report that her car was stolen," Huck said.

I flipped the visor down as we turned a corner and the sun was in my eyes. "The fire and now this. They're having bad luck," I said.

"Seems that way," Huck added. "I think—"

A car coming our way veered into our lane and then slammed on the brakes, the back end fishtailing so it blocked our way. The front of that car almost faced where it had come from. Huck stopped the police car. My head whiplashed. His gaze narrowed as he looked out the front windshield as the driver's door opened and a woman staggered out.

"Shit." His head whipped around to look me over. "You okay?"

"Yes," I murmured, my adrenaline pumping.

"Listen to me carefully. Climb out and shut your door. Stay on the ground behind the SUV so you aren't seen. Call this in." Gone was the sweet Huck. He was in police mode now, hyperfocused.

"What's going on?"

"It's Mandy. Claire's mother."

I gave the woman a quick glance, then did as Huck asked—undid my belt, opened my door, and slipped out, shutting it behind me. I took my cell and squatted down behind the rear wheel and called Graham.

Huck's door slammed. I felt the reverberations of it against my back.

"Hey, Sarah," Graham said.

"Huck and I are on County Road Four," I whispered. "A woman has blocked the road. Huck knows her and is dealing with her, but we need some help out here."

"Got it. No one's hurt?"

A gunshot had me jumping.

"Shit. You okay?"

"She doesn't know I'm here," I whispered. "Huck's talking to her, and she's got a gun. And is using it!"

"Stay down. We'll be there soon."

The line went dead, and I scrunched down and peeked under the SUV. I saw Huck's jean-clad legs. He was still standing, thank God.

"Put the gun down, Mandy."

"No way! You need to give me money. Now!"

I couldn't see the woman, but her voice was shrill.

"Why? What are you on? Meth? Put the gun down before you hurt someone."

I heard footsteps on the paved road. "That's the plan. I want you dead."

"Be pissed all you want. Shooting me won't solve anything."

How could he sound so calm? I wasn't sure if I could handle him being police chief if he dealt with people like this as part of his job.

Then I realized she wasn't part of his job. She was part of his life. The woman who'd made Claire but had fucked with him. She might be a nutjob—and dangerous—but Huck had gotten the best part of this woman. He was right. I wouldn't want to change anything that had happened because we'd never have Claire otherwise.

We just needed to get out of this alive.

"It'll solve everything. If you're dead, then Claire's mine. She inherits everything. All your Manning money."

I heard more footsteps and knew she might see me. There was a deep farmer's ditch on the side of the road. I crawled over to it, then slid down the steep bank. Glancing up, I couldn't see the road. As long as I leaned against the berm, I wouldn't be seen. I'd stay here, safe, and pray I didn't lose Huck before I ever really had him again.

―――――

HUCK

MANDY WAS A FUCKING DISASTER. I hadn't seen her in five years, and they hadn't been good to her. Her long hair was bleached but had three-inch dark roots. Her skin was pale, and she had a hideous cold sore at the corner of her mouth. It was her eyes that told me everything. She was on something. Hooked. Desperate. How she'd found an attorney to represent her was impressive, or she'd spiraled down since then.

She'd climbed from a beat-up sedan and must have been coming to the ranch. She had lady balls to stop a police car like that unless someone was having a baby or dying. She must've figured I'd be the only person driving this way in such a vehicle. The road wasn't well traveled, and she was amped. The location of the Manning ranch wasn't a secret. Anyone in the county could have given her directions.

The way she was acting, she hadn't seen Sarah. Thank fuck her focus was squarely on me. After all that Sarah had been through, she didn't need this shit. It was mine to deal with, mine to handle.

Besides, I wouldn't be able to concentrate on dealing with Mandy if Sarah was in harm's way. It was Mandy's erratic behavior and the gun she held that made her a threat. She had to be a hundred pounds soaking wet, but the gun... it fired bullets no matter who pulled the trigger. I guessed I'd have backup in about six minutes, but that was a long time.

"You think I'd leave my portion of the ranch to a five-year-old?" I called out.

Her eyes widened, and she took a step closer. Her hand wasn't steady, and that first shot had gone wide.

"She's your heir. You might not be the sperm donor, but you're on the birth certificate."

"That's right, I am. I was smart enough five years ago to get you to sign over your rights to Claire. I've been smart since, ensuring that she can't touch any of the money until she's twenty-five, and that's just a small portion."

"You'd fuck over your own daughter?" she asked, waving her arms.

"I'm saving her. She's going to know the value of hard work. Something you'll *never* understand."

I wasn't raising entitled children. They'd know the land. Respect it. If there was money, it would come second to what was important. Family. Fulfillment. Love.

"What are you going to do, Mandy? Shoot me? Then you'll be in jail and won't be able to spend a dime."

Sirens were faint in the distance. Mandy heard

em too. She started to pace, talk to herself. I mained still, hands out at my sides.

"Run, Mandy. Hear those sirens? They're for you."

I wanted her to get in her car because she'd put the un down to drive. Hopefully. We'd catch her quick nough, especially since backup was coming from wn and she'd run into them. There weren't any other ads, fields all around.

She turned to look over her shoulder, as if she ould see the police cars headed our direction. They'd e here soon.

"I hate you!" she snarled, then ran for her car. The driver's door was open, and she hopped in. I moved hen, cutting across the pavement to her passenger door. She was right-handed, so the gun had to be on the seat beside her.

I expected the engine to start and for her to peel out, but the car remained quiet. Mandy didn't. She pounded on the steering wheel and started screaming at the car. "What the fuck? Work, damn it!"

I took the opportunity with both her hands in view to yank open the door and grab the gun. It was on the seat as expected.

Two police cars raced up the straight road and blocked Mandy's car. Lights flashed as Graham and Nate, another deputy, opened their doors, squatted down behind them, and pointed their weapons.

"Clear!" I shouted. I held up the gun in my hand so they could see it as they approached.

Graham took the weapon from me as Nate moved to stand at the front bumper, gun lowered but in his hand as he focused on Mandy.

I stalked around the car and pulled her out. She barely weighed anything, her arm all skin and bones beneath my grip. She was practically feral as she clawed and resisted.

Graham joined me and helped me restrain her arms behind her back so he could cuff her. Once done, I handed her off.

"Sarah!" I shouted, spinning around toward my SUV. It was movement to my right that had me turning again. Sarah pushed herself up from the ditch and ran over. I pulled her close, hugged her fiercely.

Thank fuck she was fine. My heart was hammering.

She held something up, and I studied it. Frowned. "Is that—"

"Her starter fuse?" she asked, the corner of her mouth turning up. She tipped her head toward Mandy's car. "It was all I could do to help."

"Show me later where that is on a car, yeah?" I asked, then kissed her soundly.

"What do you want me to do with her, Chief?" Graham asked, holding a now sobbing Mandy.

"Book her. The list will include everything from reckless driving to attempted murder."

"On it," Graham replied, pushing Mandy toward his squad car. Nate followed.

I looked down at Sarah. "You okay?"

She nodded, tucked her hair back behind her ear. Her palms were dirty and so were her jeans at the knees. "You?"

I ran a hand over my face, tried to calm down. "Fuck. That was a mess. Now you've met Mandy," I said, then laughed, but there was no humor in it. "She's out of the picture for good. It's over."

"Good. Because we've got plans." She hooked her hand behind my neck and kissed the heck out of me. "I think her car's gonna need a tow. Know someone?" she asked when she finally pulled her lips from mine.

18

ARAH

IN THE END my father was called to tow Mandy's car. He was the shop on record with the department. For now. Based on the way Huck wasn't wild about my dad, that would probably change, even if I didn't set up my own business. All I knew was that I hadn't been the one to tow it. I wasn't sure if Roy had been scraped from the bottom of a liquor bottle, but I didn't care.

Huck and I had been long gone from the scene by then and settled at the station. I'd had to write up my statement about what had happened, but Alice had offered to come and collect me when I'd finished. I'd refused, even though Huck had reports of his own and l to book Mandy into custody. Being with Huck, n in the same building, was important, although I'd e to the deli down the street to get sandwiches for eryone.

We finally left around eight and stopped at my ouse—as originally planned—to get a few of my ings before heading back to the ranch. Claire hadn't un out to meet us as she had earlier, but when we went inside, we found her coming down the steps with damp hair and pale blue pajamas.

"Daddy!" she squealed, then launched herself off the third step and into his arms.

I panicked for a split second, sticking my arms out to catch her, but it was obviously a move they did often because he squeezed her close and tickled her. He made growly bear sounds and she giggled.

"You're back," she said to me once Huck stopped winding her up.

"I am. Is that okay?" I asked, setting my overnight bag down.

She nodded vigorously. "You can sleep with Daddy in his room. That's what mommies do. My friend Lizzie's mommy and daddy share a bed, and she says they make funny noises in it."

I could feel my cheeks heat, and I glanced up at Alice, who'd followed Claire down the stairs but at a slower pace. By the smile on her face, she was amused. As Huck had said, he was thirty-two years old, but still... I didn't want to be disrespectful since this was her house, too.

"I bathed and brushed and it's books time. Will you read to me, Sarah?"

My heart swelled, and I couldn't help but smile. Offering a glance at Huck, I saw the satisfaction I felt in his gaze. "I think Daddy needs to read, too."

She bounced in Huck's arms. "Yes!"

Huck set Claire down. "Go pick out two books, and we'll be right there."

She dashed up the stairs.

"I heard what happened," Alice said, her smile slipping.

"It's over," Huck told her.

She nodded once.

"It's finally time for you two to be together. I couldn't be more pleased," she said. "I'll be in my room watching my show... in case you want to make any funny noises."

I stared at her openmouthed as she walked off. "Did she just wink?"

Huck laughed. "She's been our champion all this time."

"Daddy!" Claire shouted.

He looked to me and rolled his eyes, but his expression screamed happiness instead of frustration. "We each read one book. Don't let her sucker you into more. She's smart and will try." He spoke as if the five-

year-old was a cunning legal expert. After I nodded in
—supposed—understanding, he leaned in and kissed
me. "Then you're mine. *All* mine."

Thirty minutes later Huck closed his bedroom
door behind us. He'd been right. Claire had tried
several different negotiation strategies to extend her
reading time, which impressed me. I had a feeling
she'd gotten away with it in the past, but tonight Huck
wasn't having it.

He was having me, and hopefully very soon.

Seeing him snuggled up in a single bed with
Claire, reading a book about a bear and a missing
button, definitely made my ovaries pop out a few
eggs. There was something sexy about a man with his
child.

When Huck pulled me into his arms and kissed
me, I was beyond ready. Wet, eager, and needy. Lifting
his head, he stroked my hair back and looked at me.
His pale eyes held mine.

"When I saw that gun in Mandy's hand, I panicked
about you getting hurt," he said.

"You? I was talking to Graham and heard the shot. I
thought you'd been killed!" I tried to push back and
break his hold, but he kept me snug to him.

His jaw clenched as his eyes roved over my face.
"It's over. We leave her behind, baby girl, with everything else. All we need to see is the future."

I nodded, took a deep breath. "You're right."

"I want to start that future right now." He tipped his head toward the bed. "Right there."

"Yes," I breathed, wanting that too. We'd lost six years. We'd almost lost each other today. But our time was now.

Before, we hadn't even been trying to make a baby. Now we would be. The future was finally clear.

"Yes," he repeated as he stepped back. Took my hand and led me to the side of the bed.

I burst out laughing when I saw the headboard. A wooden slat was missing right in the middle.

Huck looked to the bed and back to me. "We might need a new bed."

I shook my head, set my hands at the hem of his shirt, and started to push it up his body.

"No way. I want that there to remember the moment when we got back together."

"You want that, all you have to do is sit on my face," he countered.

We didn't say anything else after that, just stripped each other's clothes off and fell into bed together. I was beneath him, and I savored the hard press of his body. The way the hair on his chest tickled my nipples. His hand slipped between my thighs, parted me, and found me wet.

"Baby girl."

"Don't make me wait," I said, lifting my hips for him.

This was going to be a quickie. We both needed it, the connection.

He shifted, set the head of his dick at my entrance, then held himself still.

I looked up at him.

"This is it, Sarah O'Banyon soon-to-be Manning. Time to make that baby."

"Yes," I said, lifting my hips to take an inch of him into me.

He pushed the rest of the way in. "Fuck, baby girl. I'm home."

He filled me completely, and my walls rippled around him, adjusting to being filled with something so big.

He was home. Wherever he was, I belonged.

"I'm going to fuck you now, but you can't make any noises."

I giggled, my inner muscles clenching as I did so, and he groaned.

He couldn't hold back any longer and began to move. I met each thrust with my hips until we couldn't hold back our moans and groans, gasps and begging.

I came as he reached between us and pinched my clit. He plunged deep, growled. Filled me with his cum.

There was no going back now. And I wouldn't have it any other way.

———

Ready for more? Read Hand Me The Reins next!

Bought in an auction by a shy baker? No problem.
Pretending to be her boyfriend for her sister's wedding?
On it.

I can pretend all day long because I'm Thatcher
Manning, the guy who doesn't do relationships.
I'll give a woman a wild romp. Hell, I'll give her
anything. Anything but my heart.
I decided a long time ago I'd never get serious with a
woman.
The fact that I'm leaving town in a few months only
cements that decision.
But then Astrid has to get under my skin. She hands
over the reins in bed—and out—and now I'm catching
feelings.
The kind you can't fake.
Trouble is—I wasn't playing for keeps. Now, *that's* a
problem. A big one.

Read Hand Me The Reins!

BONUS CONTENT

Guess what? I've got some bonus content for you! Sign up for my mailing list. There will be special bonus content for some of my books, just for my subscribers. Signing up will let you hear about my next release as soon as it is out, too (and you get a free book...wow!)

As always...thanks for loving my books and the wild ride!

Vanessa

JOIN THE WAGON TRAIN!

If you're on Facebook, please join my closed group, the Wagon Train! Don't miss out on the giveaways and hot cowboys!

https://www.facebook.com/
groups/vanessavalewagontrain/

GET A FREE BOOK!

Join my mailing list to be the first to know of new releases, free books, special prices and other author giveaways.

http://freeromanceread.com

ABOUT VANESSA VALE

Vanessa Vale is the *USA Today* bestselling author of sexy romance novels, including her popular Bridgewater historical series and hot contemporary romances. With over one million books sold, Vanessa writes about unapologetic bad boys who don't just fall in love, they fall hard. Her books are available worldwide in multiple languages in e-book, print, audio and even as an online game. When she's not writing, Vanessa savors the insanity of raising two boys and figuring out how many meals she can make with a pressure cooker. While she's not as skilled at social media as her kids, she loves to interact with readers.